CAPTURING
JESSICA

CAPTURING JESSICA

by

Jane Hardee

2016

CAPTURING JESSICA

ISBN 13: 978-1-62639-836-8

This Trade Paperback Original Is Published By
Bold Strokes Books, Inc.
P.O. Box 249
Valley Falls, NY 12185

First Edition: December 2016

CREDITS
EDITOR: KATIA NOYES
PRODUCTION DESIGN: STACIA SEAMAN
COVER DESIGN BY JEANINE HENNING

Acknowledgments

This is my first novel, and I was incredibly overwhelmed by the process of editing. A huge and well-deserved thank you to my editor, Katia Noyes, for her insight, knowledge, patience, kindness and sense of humor. I am forever indebted to her for the resources, knowledge, and time she spent helping me beat this novel into submission. Editing was a strange new world for me, but I had the most capable and understanding tour guide. Thank you for all of your late-night and early-morning emails, all of the links and book suggestions, and of course all of the hahas. I look forward to working with you again.

Thank you to everyone I worked with from Bold Strokes Books during this process—Sandy Lowe, Cindy Cresap, Ruth Sternglantz, and Kim Baldwin. I appreciate your knowledge and assistance.

A special thanks in advance to those who read this story. I have spent countless hours reading and rereading lesbian fiction, and I love to disappear into a place where I have never been with people I have never met. If you are able to escape into the world and characters I have created even for a little while, then I feel like I have been successful.

For Crystal, who bought me my first romance novel.

CHAPTER ONE

Michael threw her arm over her face to block the rays of sunlight streaming through the hotel window and with her other hand fumbled to silence her phone on the nightstand. She guessed it must be nearing noon. The sleeping woman next to her felt warm and soft pressed against her back, but Michael felt trapped. She peeled the woman's small hand away from her body, threw her legs over the side of the bed, and sat up.

Glancing around the room, Michael wondered about the paint-by-number artwork. Why couldn't budget hotels get reprints of quality art? It would help draw attention away from their drab carpeting and outdated fixtures. As quietly as she could, Michael reached for her briefs and jeans. Although in light of last night, she felt silly for not wanting to be seen naked.

"That's not your girlfriend blowing up your phone, is it?" The woman rolled over onto her stomach, giving Michael a great view of her ass. *Ally?* Yes, that was her name.

"No. No girlfriend," Michael said, yanking her jeans all the way up her thighs. She grabbed her shirt and walked to the window, wanting to get some space. Pulling the curtain aside, she surveyed the Atlanta skyline and the small parking lot below the second-floor window. The display on her phone read four missed calls and three messages. She wished there was a balcony so she could step outside for some privacy.

"Yes, it's me again," she heard Camille's irritated voice say. Before listening to the rest, Michael pressed the callback button.

"Where the hell have you been?" Camille said. "You better have that sculpture finished by Friday." About three or four days before one of Michael's projects was due, Camille turned into a drill sergeant. Michael wasn't worried. She was fast becoming known as the sculptor to hire in Georgia if you wanted a realistic carving of a strong, gorgeous woman. Michael knew she was talented, but she also knew her success wouldn't have happened without Camille's connections and shrewd business sense. Somewhere between Camille bitching about timelines and finishing touches, Michael was relieved to hear Ally get up and go into the bathroom.

"Relax. I'm on it." Michael didn't want to sound curt, but Camille knew she always kept on schedule with her work so the guilt trip was unnecessary. With more annoyance, she realized that she hadn't put on her bra. Staring at the closed bathroom door, she strode to the other side of the bed and pocketed her sports bra. "And when am I late on a project anyway?"

"Never, thanks to me. I'll be by your loft later this week to check on your progress."

"Fine." As she ended the call, Michael felt the back pocket of her jeans for her keys and wallet, anxious to get any awkward good-byes over.

Ally pranced out of the small bathroom wearing a big T-shirt and pulling her long, red curls into a messy bun. "I can tell you're itching to leave, and I've got a flight to catch." Ally stepped aside to let Michael get to the door. "It was…tons of fun."

Michael grabbed the door handle.

"You don't talk much do you, sugar?"

"You're not the first to notice." Michael gave her a quick peck on the lips and pulled open the door.

Of course she jumped into bed with Ally. It helped keep her thoughts at bay. *Damn.* Now the memories came back. Vivid images of Jess on the arm of some woman from the night before flashed before her eyes. Who was that butch chick anyway? She looked as if she crawled out of an Abercrombie & Fitch ad, strong men's cologne and all. Michael had never seen her at Nine's Bar before, and she was hoping not to bump into her again.

❖

Last night had started well at least. Michael's buddies gathered downtown at Nine's, just as they did every Friday night.

"And then she pulls me into the stall and sticks her hand down my pants! I know, hard to believe, right?" Morgan's high ponytail whipped around her head during her animated storytelling. "She only lasted three days before Ted fired her. Said she couldn't make coffee worth a damn. Now he thinks it's my job to get his coffee." She rolled her eyes in annoyance. "What a prick."

"Wait a minute," Camille said, arching an eyebrow, "you get his coffee for him?"

"Hell no, I don't. It doesn't say barista on my fucking resume." Morgan blew out a long whistle, seeming ready to change the topic even though she brought it up.

"I can't believe you still work for that guy, Morgan," Jess said.

A tiny crease formed between Jess's eyebrows, and she caught her bottom lip in her teeth. It was impossible for

Michael to catalog all of Jess's expressions because she was so empathetic. Feelings were as natural as breathing to this woman. Jess thrived on connecting with people, especially through emotion. She had a different expression for every situation. Sometimes Michael lost track of all conversation and watched Jess's face move and change. She imagined the first viewers of silent films, completely captivated and spellbound, without need for any dialogue or even noticing its absence. As her imagination wandered further, she could see Jess in grainy black-and-white film, with her eyes open wide and lips pursed, as suitors piled gifts in front of her.

When Morgan shrugged, Jess stuck out her tongue in disgust, and this drew Michael's attention to the curves of her mouth. Her lips sparkled with a kissable shade of light pink gloss. *Maybe it's fruit flavored.*

"He's such a jerk. And that was two," Jess said, scowling at Morgan. As an elementary school teacher, Jess's vocabulary consisted of PG-rated language, and she kept tabs on Morgan's use of curse words. If she got to twenty, Morgan had to pay Jess's tab. Jess made a face of disapproval at Morgan's halfhearted apology.

As an excuse to stare at Jess, Michael pulled the permanent marker from her pocket and began a rough sketch of Jess's profile on a square cocktail napkin. The group was used to Michael's obsessive sketching of people, and she knew it wouldn't draw much attention.

"If I want to make partner someday, I have to stick with it. But if he does keep asking me to make his *frigging* coffee," Morgan said, staring at Jess, "I may have to put some rat poison in it. Where do you buy that anyway?" Morgan pulled on her ponytail to tighten it closer to her scalp. Michael assumed that for Morgan, being one of the most successful female attorneys in Atlanta and working with a bunch of sexist dickheads was a fair trade. Michael broke eye contact with Jess's face to look at Morgan's business suit, a stark contrast to her sporty ponytail. She'd ditched her classy up-do the minute she sat down. Morgan was the last to arrive at nearly ten thirty, having just come from her office. Michael admired Morgan's drive, but she preferred being in control of her own schedule. Working alone suited her as well.

"I know. I just hate that you have to put up with that." Jess wouldn't know about having trouble with coworkers. Everyone loved Jess. Michael made small, quick lines to emphasize the sympathetic furrow in Jess's brows and the pronounced Cupid's bow of her upper lip. Michael felt in her element, content to sketch and listen to the others.

"Who is that tall drink of water over there?" Camille popped the olive of her martini in her mouth and pointed toward the bar with her cocktail pick. Pausing, Michael made a show of pretending to stretch her arms and yawn, resting one on the back of the booth behind Jess to look around at the bar.

"Real slick," Morgan said.

Jess laughed. Michael loved that spontaneous giggle and couldn't help but respond with a wicked grin. Jess's eyes sparkled when she saw Michael's expression, and she laughed some more. Michael loved the way that they didn't need words to communicate.

Knowing Camille's interest in more masculine women, Michael wasn't concerned about impressing anyone with her less-than-subtle move. She liked her women as far on the feminine end of the spectrum as she could get them. Michael's eyes settled on the woman she hadn't seen at Nine's before. The woman's biceps flexed under her expensive button-down shirt when she pointed to the top-shelf brands behind the bar. Michael took pride in her own well-formed arms and shoulders, the result of countless hours of sculpting and lifting stone, but one look at this chick and she could tell her physique came with a pricey trainer and many curls in front of a mirror.

"Never seen her before." Uninterested, Michael returned her attention to her sketch. She angled her marker slightly to capture the wisps of hair on Jess's forehead that had escaped her barrette.

"Is she cute?" Jess craned her neck to look at the woman.

"Why don't you just stand up and point at her, Jess," Morgan said, poking her in the ribs.

Michael used the hand she had left on the back of the booth to straighten Jess's head so she could continue to sketch her. "Hold still."

Almost as if she had heard them, the woman picked up her drink and headed straight for their corner booth.

"Good evenin', ladies. I'm Dana."

She spoke with what Michael guessed was an exaggerated Southern drawl and extended her hand to Jess. Now the woman had Michael's full attention. Camille and Morgan were closest to her. Why the hell would she reach over the table like a dumbass to shake Jess's hand first? Michael's arm shot out to push Jess's chin up slightly as she continued to sketch, but she kept her eyes locked on the newcomer as she attempted to stake her nonexistent claim on Jess.

Jess kept her head in position, but put her hand out to shake Dana's. "Jess. My pleasure."

"Hey, Dana," Morgan interjected as Dana and Jess shook hands, not trying in the slightest to hide her interest. "I'm Morgan. This is Camille, and here's Van Gogh. Why don't you join us?" She motioned for Camille to move farther into the booth.

"Thanks, I'd love to." Her eyes never left Jess, even as she shook hands with Camille and Morgan.

"Haven't seen you in here before. New to Atlanta?" Morgan asked.

"Just moved from Dallas. Needed a change of scenery, I guess you might say."

Must be code for I was an asshole to my last girlfriend. Michael tried not to smirk.

"Is our little town suiting you okay so far?" At that moment Michael was grateful for Camille's sexy voice since it drew Toolbag's attention away from Jess.

"It's great. Not that dissimilar from Dallas. A little bit of country in the city." After a few minutes of exchanging pleasantries, Dana scooted out of the booth. She eyed Jess and drawled, "Would you like to dance, darlin'?"

"I'd love to."

Dana took Jess's hand as Morgan stood up to let Jess out of the booth. Jess glanced back at Michael's sketch, then at Camille and Morgan. "Are you girls coming?"

"I need another drink first." Morgan plopped back down in the booth, and Dana and Jess headed to the dance floor. The bored look on Camille's face told Michael she wasn't too bummed about missing a dance with Ms. Lone Star.

"I don't like her," Michael said. She folded the sketch of Jess and put it and the marker in her back pocket.

"Pssh, what's not to like? She's gorgeous. And Jess agrees with me." Morgan gestured over her shoulder toward Dana and Jess dancing together.

Camille looked over at Michael with a knowing glare. Michael glared back, indicating she wanted Camille to keep her lips sealed. Camille was the only person who knew Michael's true feelings for Jess. She picked up signs everyone else seemed to miss, including any signs Michael tried to conceal.

Camille and Michael had met at one of Michael's first gallery shows in Atlanta shortly after she graduated from Savannah College of Art and Design. They clicked instantly. They became lovers for about three minutes and then decided they would make better friends. Camille disliked Michael's inability to be truly intimate. Camille joked that Michael was better with stone women than real ones.

After Morgan headed to the bar to get another drink, Michael thanked Camille for her silence. Camille looked at Michael with sympathetic eyes and stroked her hand. "No need to say another word."

Michael never had been a big talker. Even as a child she rarely began conversations with classmates and only responded when necessary. She attributed this to the fact that her mother talked all the time, so from a young age she learned that the only time she needed to speak was if it was important.

She resisted the urge to search out Jess and Toolbag on the dance floor for as long as she could, then her eyes darted around until they found the two of them. In Michael's opinion, they danced a little too closely considering this was a fast song and they had just met. She watched the easy smile that came to Jess's lips when Dana leaned down to say something close to her ear. Dana put her hands on Jess's hips and then spun her around. Soon Jess draped her arms loosely around Dana's neck. Jealousy caused Michael's face to heat, and she jumped up to follow Morgan to the bar. She needed something stronger than the light beer she had been nursing.

Michael walked to the end of the bar farthest from the dance floor and held up a hand to Robin, the only bartender. "Tequila shot."

Licking her hand and grabbing the salt shaker, Michael concentrated on the task to avoid searching out Jess again. Her frustration mounted as she thought of Dana's hands roaming over Jess's body. She downed the first of what she knew would be a few shots.

As she turned to ask Robin for another, she noticed an attractive petite redhead sitting alone at the end of the bar eyeing her. Her scarlet fingernails played with the label on her beer. When she tilted her head, the light caught on the small stud in her nostril. The pendant around her neck also sparkled and emphasized the deep neckline of her dress. Michael met and held her gaze.

The woman grabbed her drink and sauntered toward Michael through the throng of people.

"Is this seat taken?" She pointed to the unoccupied stool next to Michael.

"It is now," Michael said, gesturing for her to sit. She took the woman's cool hand into hers. "Michael."

"Ally," the woman replied, close to Michael's ear.

A pleasant shot of desire went straight to her groin as the woman breathed against her ear. When searching out female company, Michael preferred woman who were direct like herself.

"I'm in town on business." Ally slipped a finger through the belt loop on Michael's baggy jeans and tugged. "You live in Atlanta?"

"Home sweet home. What does the rest of your evening look like?" Michael asked, wearing her most devilish grin and pushing all thoughts of Jess from her mind. "Because I'm ready to get out of here."

Turning slightly so the woman was now sitting between her legs, Michael rested a hand on Ally's hip. Michael drew small circles on the soft fabric of Ally's dress with her finger and watched her pupils dilate. Feeling confident she had secured company for the night, Michael stood to her full height, towering over Ally, and placed some bills on the counter.

At Ally's hotel, Michael was treated to a striptease as she sat on the edge of the full bed. Hips swaying, Ally pulled the hem of her dress up a few inches to reveal a substantial tattoo of a blossoming cherry tree and a nice view of her thigh-high stockings, held up by a black garter belt. Michael swallowed in anticipation. Michael shoved the dress higher, interested to see where the tattoo ended. Once the dress joined her high heels on the floor, Ally stepped forward and placed her hands on Michael's shoulders.

"You like ink?" Ally ran her hands from Michael's biceps up to the back of her neck.

Michael stroked Ally's thighs, her fingers indenting the smooth flesh. The pale skin with the bright, colorful ink created a striking contrast. *Damn it. Where is my sketchpad when I need it?*

"I like thighs," Michael whispered. Ally's hips and ass were rounded, leading to firm muscular legs. *Fuck thigh gap.*

Michael wanted those supple legs wrapped around her hips, her stomach, her face.

"I like broad shoulders. And firm muscles." Ally rubbed Michael's shoulders again as she straddled her, shoving her back down on the bed. "And I like being in charge."

"Yours to command." Michael's arousal increased as she thought about submitting to whatever Ally wanted to take from her.

Michael was not disappointed. Ally had indeed been amazing. They spent the better part of the night pleasuring each other, figuring out what the other liked and responded to. Ally knew what she wanted and had no qualms about bossing Michael around.

❖

When Michael hopped into her old Scout the next morning, she turned the radio up loud, loud enough to blast away any worries about where Jess spent the night. She tried not to think of Jess at all. It would only make her angry. She should be able to think about her best friend without being overcome with a hollow feeling in her chest. Then on top of that, there was the grueling charade of pretending that she didn't want to throttle every cologne-wearing, tailored-shirted, bicep-curling moron on the planet. Was that the kind of woman Jess wanted? Someone surface level with no ambition or character?

She spent every day convincing herself she was fine with unrequited love. *We are best friends. That's my story, and I'm sticking to it.* Camille often asked why she didn't come clean and tell Jess the truth. No way in hell was that going to happen. The most obvious reason being that Jess did not return her feelings. She was her best friend, and Michael wanted to keep it that way. If she told Jess the truth, she'd be shot down and lose her best friend in one dumbass move. No, she and Jess would remain best friends, and Michael would continue to bury her feelings in hopes of someday having them disappear.

CHAPTER TWO

W ill you please tell her I called again? This is Ms. Gable, Alex's teacher. Thank you." Jess hung up and tossed Alex's folder on her desk.

It was the fourth time in as many days that she had tried to get in touch with one of Alex's parents. Were they not getting her messages, or were they ignoring their son's progress and education? Alex was a six-year-old boy with autism. Jess tried not to play favorites with her students, but there was something about the way he smiled and interacted with adults, always wanting to please. He was a special kid, and Jess wanted to see him succeed in school. Alex was from a wealthy family, and his stay-at-home mom spent a lot of time at one of Atlanta's most elite country clubs. She must be very busy with tennis if she couldn't return a simple phone call from her child's special education teacher.

Jess knew many parents had a difficult time accepting their child's disability, but she was a firm believer that you needed to face obstacles and deal with them head-on. It was important for parents to get as much information as possible and learn what was going to help their child be successful. These were their children, for goodness sake, and they needed to take part in their education. She had dealt with difficult students in her early years of teaching when she worked with kids with behavioral disorders, and Alex was not the toughest she had seen. He was a sweet, hardworking boy who wanted nothing more than to learn. Why was his education not a priority to his parents?

She put aside her anger and packed up for the night. When she walked to her car at nearly five o'clock, the parking lot was almost empty. Her coworkers were always telling her she needed to leave work earlier. Piling her books and papers in the backseat, she climbed into the front of her Passat.

Because she hadn't spoken with Michael since Friday night, Jess decided to take a right out of the parking lot and head to Michael's loft. She hadn't spoken to Dana either, and Jess wasn't surprised she hadn't called. After exchanging numbers, she had made it clear to Dana that sleeping together was out of the question. She had become tired of women wanting to sleep with her rather than forming some kind of relationship first. Jess snorted. Not that it happened that often. She had been out of the closet since her senior year of high school and had yet to feel a deep romantic connection. Jess dated in college, but those few sexual experiences left her feeling unsatisfied, and these days, the intimacy of sex was something she didn't want to share with just anyone. Sure she felt the desire for sex, but she wasn't desperate. After all, she could take care of things herself.

At the bar on Friday, Dana made some excuse to Jess about having to get up early for work, but when Jess returned to her friends, she later saw Dana leave on the arm of some skinny skank, a woman who looked like she hadn't eaten a cupcake in her entire life. It irritated Jess that she wasn't worth Dana's time because they wouldn't be sleeping together. She had tried to be polite when declining Dana's offer to go back to her hotel. What happened to just getting to know someone, seeing where things went? She was not the jumping-into-bed type, and she never would be.

The Atlanta traffic moved at an even slower rate than normal, and she felt exhausted and on edge from her parent calls. Stuck behind an eighteen-wheeler on I-285, Jess scanned the radio channels for something upbeat, something to help her get out of her funk. Seeing Michael always made her feel better when she was feeling down about anything, even work problems. She thought about her best friend and the many nights they had shared and talked about their troubles. Their friendship ebbed and flowed through the years, but they were always there for each other.

The night before Michael left for college, Jess had come out to her. Michael had been out of the closet herself for several years by then and Jess felt comfortable confiding in her. Their friendship was strong, but Jess feared when they graduated their ties might loosen. After telling Michael she was gay, Jess had been so desperate to solidify and validate their friendship that she impulsively asked Michael to sleep with her. She could think of no other way to permanently bind herself to Michael and make sure she wouldn't be forgotten. Michael refused but had been kind enough not to make Jess feel stupid for suggesting such a thing. They never spoke of it again, and despite Jess's fears, their friendship stood the test of time. After college, they both came back to Atlanta and spoke every day. It was a strong bond, and she considered Michael one of the most important people in her life.

Jess stopped for pizza, knowing that Michael would be working on her latest project and so engrossed that she might forget to eat. She rode the freight elevator up to Michael's loft and pulled out her key. They had shared keys to each other's apartments for years, and Michael's new loft was no different. Her home was a beautiful place with exposed brick walls and floor-to-ceiling windows on one side. It was an old factory building that had been turned into four identical lofts many years after the factory closed and had a great view of the Atlanta skyline but was far from the chaos of downtown. Michael gave the loft a lot of personal touches to make the large modern space feel homier: mismatched, overstuffed couches and chairs in the living room area; a large, country-style pine dining table; and favorite artwork by female artists on the walls. Michael's studio was in the back corner near the windows, the best place for natural light.

It was hard for Jess to believe how modern the loft felt inside, since the outside hallway still had exposed studs and rusted ironwork. She pulled the elevator gate open with one hand, balancing the pizza and her purse in the other. The large elevator was one of the reasons Michael chose the live/work loft. She no longer needed to rent a studio space because she could have large media like stone and plaster delivered. Jess heard loud music playing, walked in, and set the pizza down.

A large plastic tarp hung from the ceiling to keep Michael's studio separate from the living area and prevent her furniture from being covered in dust and debris. Jess pulled back the tarp to find Michael working with a chisel and large hammer. Before Jess looked at the sculpture, she watched Michael in action. She bent at an angle to work, and her broad shoulders tensed as she held a chisel in place and pounded it with a steel hammer. Chunks of stone fell to the floor around her feet, but she took no notice. Michael insisted on working barefoot, and below her long khaki shorts, dust covered her feet and calves. Watching Michael work, it occurred to Jess why she stayed so muscular without working out. When she sat back on her haunches, Michael's biceps became more pronounced as she made more precise chips in the stone.

Jess wondered about the stark differences in their bodies.

She envied Michael's defined physique, as she herself was on the short side of average and rather curvaceous with large breasts. There was a time when she had been attracted to Michael, but that was just a schoolgirl crush. After all, Michael had been the only lesbian she knew. When her eyes settled on Michael's well-shaped rear, she swallowed and cleared her throat. She reminded herself that the importance of their friendship outweighed any possible physical attraction.

Michael turned around. She lifted her face mask and grinned, then pulled a dusty rag from her pocket and wiped her hands. "What do you think?" Jess got distracted by the trickle of sweat sliding down Michael's neck and took a moment to answer. There was something sexy about a woman who worked up a sweat, to see her so engrossed in what she was doing that she forgot everything else.

"No comment?" Michael raised the towel to dry the sweat from her neck and face and ducked past Jess to turn down the stereo.

"It looks fantastic," Jess said, turning back to the sculpture to keep her eyes off Michael's body. What was wrong with her? It had been years since she'd thought of Michael that way. She followed Michael to the kitchen area and tried to act normally. *Just think about something else.*

"Hawaiian Special!" Michael opened the box and inhaled the scent of pizza.

Jess found two beers in the fridge and pulled two plates from the open shelving. She placed a plate in front of Michael just as she took a bite of pizza and plunked on a bar stool.

"Thanks. What would I do without you?" Michael said, chewing a mouthful of pizza.

"Probably starve." Jess came around the counter and sat near Michael, but avoided her eyes.

"School okay? You didn't bring too much home, did

you?" Michael often told Jess she worked too hard, yet Jess knew it was also one of the things she admired about her.

"The kids are great. It's just the parents. I don't even want to think about them." Jess put down her pizza and rubbed her temples.

"Sure. What do you want to talk about? Anything going on this weekend?"

"Actually, I have been meaning to ask you a favor," Jess said. She had been putting off this discussion.

"I should have known you wouldn't get the Hawaiian Special without asking for something. Spit it out." Michael took a long swallow of beer.

Jess placed her hand on Michael's arm and instantly regretted it. Her tan skin was soft and still damp with sweat. And she could feel the hard muscle underneath. Clearing her throat, she pulled her hand away. "I want you to come with me to Stevie's birthday party Friday night." The muscle Jess was just admiring tensed.

"Nah, I've got a lot going on," Michael said, jerking her chin toward her work area and indicating her nearly finished sculpture.

"Come on, please," Jess begged. Michael had always been standoffish with Stevie. Jess couldn't figure out why because Stevie was funny and fun to be around. She could be a little flirty at times, and immature, but for the most part Jess thought she was a good person. "I really want you there. And you guys have never really had a chance to get to know each other."

"Maybe another time."

"Michael, please...for me?" Jess said, hoping her voice sounded sweet and innocent. She attempted to make puppy dog eyes.

Michael elbowed her in the ribs, giving a lopsided smile. "Fine," she said with a groan. "Count me in."

❖

Wiping her brow with the back of her hand, Michael stepped back to examine her sculpture's lips. A few more touches and she would be complete. A group of well-known female doctors had commissioned her current project for their new office on Decatur Street. They wanted a dramatic sculpture for their lobby, and Michael's realistic and contemporary style fit the bill. She'd made them a limestone statue of a beautiful nude woman, standing tall and proud, feminine but not too delicate, and her expression brooding. The facial features showed determination; the brow was furrowed, and the mouth, pursed.

It was important for Michael to portray strong personality and believability in all her pieces. She wanted them to come to life. Her sculptures varied in size, shape, and medium, but Michael had a knack for capturing realistic facial expressions and postures. One gallery owner commented that most of her sculptures sported "resting bitch face." That was fine with her. She hated works that portrayed women as docile, delicate, weak creatures. Michael often finished her female sculptures with a claw-chisel to give them a rougher, less refined look. Unlike most sculptors, Michael did not need clay models of her work to reference as she sculpted. Her professor at the Savannah College of Art and Design had hated this and required as part of her grade that she create models. Michael kept the models in the corner as she worked, much to his annoyance. Michael learned early that her hands and fingers did most of the carving and not her eyes.

Placing the hammer and chisel in her tool belt, she looked into the statue's eyes. She liked to feel connected to her work, as if she knew the form, and the form knew her as well. Michael stepped back and looked at the statue from head to toe. She ran her hands over the torso and legs and face. Something didn't feel right. The expression looked softer than she had intended. This wasn't a woman she recognized. This woman was a pensive stranger. She was waiting for something, brooding.

This happened more often these days. She sought to create something beautiful, yet when finished realized that the work reflected a deep restlessness. Things were going great, and she was getting more commissions all the time. What did she have to be restless about? Maybe the word wasn't restless. Maybe it was lonely. No, that wasn't it either. *It's not loneliness... it's Jess-less-ness. I'm pathetic.* Michael felt an urge to chisel the face right off the sculpture's head. Instead she grabbed the broom leaning against her work table and vigorously swept the debris left from hours of sculpting.

As promised, Camille stopped by to check on Michael's progress, but Michael wasn't ready to show it quite yet, so Camille brought up Michael's new plans for the weekend.

"But why the hell did you agree to go? You hate Stevie. Every time she gets near Jess you look like you want to crack a beer bottle over her head."

"That's because I do," Michael said, hiding in her studio behind the tarp. She didn't want to talk about her jealousy. She could not stand Stevie. Like Dana, she was a good-looking, cocky lesbian who hit on anyone with big boobs. Especially Jess. It was one thing for Michael to watch Jess get hit on by a total stranger. It was something completely different for her to subject herself to a night of torture watching someone touch and flirt with Jess. It was hard for Michael not to laugh when Jess suggested that she and Stevie get to know each other. The only reason they had never had a conversation of more than three sentences was because Stevie was constantly trying to get into Jess's pants. It was Jess's final plea that had convinced her.

Michael, please...for me?

Michael both loved and hated it when Jess said her name. It was so sweet to hear her name leave those beautiful lips, but it came with a reminder that Jess would never say her name in a more intimate way. A way she had dreamed of for so many years. As she looked into those big blue eyes, her resolve had crumbled.

Michael stopped sweeping and peeked at Camille from her studio. "I agreed to go because..."

Camille returned from the kitchen area with two glasses of wine. "Because you're madly in love with her, and you worship the ground she walks on, and you would do anything for her?" Camille said in a rush, as she sat down on Michael's big red couch and tucked her legs beneath her.

"Something like that." Michael dumped the dust pan in the large trash can and came from behind the tarp and joined Camille on the couch.

Michael wondered if it was as obvious to Jess that she was being jealous and overprotective. Sure she was protective of all her friends and would do anything for them, but with Jess it was different, almost like she wanted to shield her from a world of unruly, sex-starved lesbians. It was almost...chauvinist. Jess could take care of herself, but that didn't change the fact that Michael wanted to be near her side.

Thinking back, she had felt protective of Jess since the day they met. The first day of seventh grade Michael had missed the bus home, enjoying walking, even in the heat of August. As she passed Mrs. Clark's yard, she heard someone yelling from the other side of the hedges. She ducked down and approached the bushes. Michael peered around and noticed a girl standing against the brick wall of the house. Jackson and Jared Akers stood in front of her. She hated those guys. They picked on everyone, even though they got bullied themselves by the high-school kids. Shoulders squared, Michael strode over to Jackson, the older of the two, and crossed her arms. Michael had hit her adult height of five foot ten by the time she was twelve, and she towered over Jackson by at least two inches.

"Get out of here, Shafer, this is none of your damn business," Jackson said. "We're just playing with the new girl, but the dumb bitch keeps screaming like a baby." Michael never figured out if it was the fact that Jess looked so scared with tears streaming down her face or if it was the use of the word "bitch" that made her snap. Before another coherent thought entered her brain, she reared back and punched Jackson in the face. To this day, it was the best right cross she ever threw. She walked Jess home every day after that.

"You could tell her, you know." She was startled by Camille's words, having been deep in thought.

"What, so we could be another lesbian, friends-to-lovers casualty? No. She is my best friend. I wouldn't ruin that for anything."

"Hey, we escaped that fate," Camille said, referring to their romantic history.

Michael smirked. "You weren't that good in bed."

Camille threw a couch pillow at Michael's face. "I can't help it if you're not my type."

"Now you tell me."

"Seriously, if you ever need to talk, I'm here. Any time. I can tell how hard this is."

Michael ran her hands through her hair. It was getting harder. Harder to ignore these feelings. Harder not to hate everyone who touched Jess. Harder not to pull Jess into her arms and kiss her senseless every time they were in the same room. And her smell. Either Michael's sense of smell was getting better with age, or Jess's scent was. It was the freshest, cleanest smell she had ever known. Jess never smelled fake or flowery. It was a simple smell that suited her. When Jess sat close to her, or leaned near her to tell her something, the scent invaded Michael's brain and stayed with her for hours.

Michael knew Camille meant well, but didn't want to talk more about Jess. Instead she focused on one thing she could control. "Ready to see her?"

"I thought you'd never ask."

Michael pinned back the tarp and unveiled her new sculpture. "It's not quite done but will be by tomorrow."

"Wow. As long as being lovelorn doesn't interfere with your ability to sculpt a pissed-off, sexy woman, your career sure isn't in danger. If anything, I'd say it's helping." Camille winked. "She seems to be your muse."

CHAPTER THREE

How could she have a closet full of clothes and nothing to wear? Jess scoffed at her reflection in the full-length mirror and tugged off the fourth pair of jeans she had tried. She threw them on the bed in the reject pile, getting larger by the minute. Looking in the mirror over her shoulder as she buttoned them, she settled on another pair of dark denim jeans. The promising tag read "Instantly Slims You." Next she went into the bathroom, wearing only her jeans and bra, to finish her makeup. She loved this simple black lace bra. *What a shame no one will see it.* Shaking her head and dismissing the thought, she reached inside her makeup bag.

As she carefully applied her mascara, she decided it was a good night to wear her mother's pearls, given to her the day she left for college. Her mother loved their classic elegance and liked to remind Jess that pearls could be worn with either casual jeans or a cocktail dress. Jess missed having her mother's advice. Beatrice Gable had been a strong role model, the most important person in her life. She died from a stroke during Jess's junior year at Florida State University. It came as a sudden and unbelievable shock. Yet, the truth was, it happened exactly the way Beatrice would have wanted. She was never one to draw things out or beat around the bush.

Jess, of course, was devastated. Besides her older sister

Sara, her mother was her only family. All she could think about at the time was that her mother would never see her graduate or get married. She would never again have her mother's shoulder to cry on, have her unconditional support. Later, she realized the tragedy was not hers alone. How young and healthy her mother had been and how much more she still had to offer the world. At fifty-two, she was nowhere near ready to "meet her maker," as she used to say. For months Jess dragged though her days. She had never cried so many tears.

Pulling on her shirt as she walked out of the bathroom, Jess wondered how she ever got through that year. Her heart warmed remembering how Michael had taken a week off from her own studies at SCAD to comfort and stay with her. If it wasn't for Michael, Jess didn't know if she could have survived her grief. Jess had always cherished their friendship, but it was during that difficult period that Michael became a vital part of her life. Michael made her remember that she had a home and that even though her mother was gone, she still had family, a family with Michael in Atlanta and with her sister, Sara, in New York. She wasn't alone and still had people who cared for her. Michael helped Jess take comfort in knowing that she would always be loved. That fact was unshakeable.

Jess glanced at the clock. 6:47. *Crap.* She was late for Stevie's birthday party. Taking the top off her perfume, she sprayed her neck and wrists, hurried through the kitchen, searched for her keys, and tore down the hallway, struggling to put on her new black flats.

❖

Nine's Bar was never crowded on Friday nights. They usually had the best crowd on Wednesdays and Saturdays. If Michael was ever in the mood to meet a good-looking woman, she wouldn't come on Friday, but tonight looked like a good crowd with quite a few patrons seated at the bar, as well as at the low, circular tables. The owner was a straight, older man who had some interesting ideas about what the décor of a gay bar should look like. There were the traditional promotional posters for drag performances stapled haphazardly to the wall, along with ads from Atlanta's local LGBT newspaper. Twinkling Christmas lights hung from the ceiling and several stiletto heels on the bar read "tips" in sparkly letters. The top level served as more seating for the bar, and several wide steps lead to the lower level with more tables and mismatched chairs. The strange, iridescent lavender dance floor served as a stage on drag nights and a curtain led to the backstage area. Michael scanned the crowd looking for familiar faces and sauntered up to the bar and ordered a beer.

"That's three dollars, honey." Robin set the bottle on the counter and winked.

"Start me a tab." Michael knew this was going to be a long night. She took a long pull from the bottle and noticed Morgan striding toward her with a half-empty drink in her hand.

"Been here long?" Michael gestured to the open seat, and Morgan slid onto the stool next to where Michael was leaning.

"My second drink already. Rough week. My brainless boss can't understand that even though I have tits, I also manage to have a brain."

"Well, you know how…" Michael caught sight of Jess walking through the door. Her brown hair was cut into a bob style, but tonight it had long, gentle waves, and Michael wished she could run her hands through it. Jess smiled at the doorman as he checked her ID. She had a small barrette securing her long bangs and wore what Michael recognized as her mother's pearls. Her simple makeup emphasized her eyes. Michael moved her own eyes down Jess's body. A fitted black shirt with some sort of frilly pink flower thing on the neckline accentuated her perfect breasts. And those jeans. Damn. Michael hadn't ever seen Jess in those before. They hugged her curves in all the right places. Michael favored hips and thighs to any other part on a woman's body, and those jeans reminded her why. Jess oozed femininity. She looked beautiful.

"Hello?" Morgan waved a hand in front of Michael's face. "You know how *what?*"

Michael swatted at her hand playfully, relieved that Morgan had not noticed where her attention had been diverted. "Yeah, you know how some men are."

"It's a man's world," Morgan said, sarcastically imitating a deep macho voice.

Michael felt bad for Morgan. She had worked twice as hard in college as her male peers, and when she entered the workforce, she competed with them again for the same jobs. Now she had secured a position but still experienced discrimination.

"Hey, there's Jess." Morgan jumped off her stool to greet her.

As if I hadn't noticed. After saying hello and giving Morgan a quick hug, Jess came closer. Michael tried not to gasp as Jess put her arms around her neck.

Putting her mouth next to Michael's ear to prevent Morgan from overhearing, Jess whispered, "Thank you for coming. I owe you."

Michael ached when Jess's body pressed against hers. She put her hands on Jess's shoulders to avoid grabbing her hips. "No problem."

Jess turned her attention to Morgan and asked how work was going. Michael wished she could slow her heartbeat and avoided making eye contact with Jess. This night was going to be endless.

By the time Stevie and several of her friends arrived around eight, Michael was on her fourth beer. If she had to endure Stevie Balford, she was not going to do it sober.

They made their way to a large corner booth that Stevie had reserved for the evening. Morgan trailed behind with Michael and didn't seem excited about the evening either.

"I wonder what bullshit we are going to have to listen to tonight," Morgan said. She was not one of Stevie's biggest fans, though Michael could never figure out why. A sexy butch was usually right up Morgan's alley. Stevie was a strong, good-looking, successful lesbian who volunteered as a firefighter in her spare time. *A real superwoman!* She was charismatic and made people feel at ease when she spoke with them. All those were qualities Michael could find attractive in a woman, but not when paired with a humongous ego.

What most bothered Michael was the predatory way Stevie looked at Jess. And the unwelcome flirting. At least, Michael thought it was unwelcome. They had never talked about it before, but Michael was almost positive Jess did not return Stevie's affections. She rarely hung out with Stevie alone, and at times, Jess seemed uncomfortable with her. Why Stevie continued to try and impress her was beyond Michael. *Probably can't take the blow to her inflated ego.*

❖

The next few hours were tolerable enough. Jess positioned herself away from Stevie to try and deflect her flirting to other women at the table. It seemed to be working, and Jess spent much of the evening talking to Morgan and Michael, and enjoyed herself a lot more than she had expected. Conversation flowed between the three of them, and Stevie interjected only occasionally. Jess stopped after two cocktails, even though it was Friday. She knew Morgan had been drinking for some time, and she wanted to be able to drive her home.

It was almost midnight when the DJ cut off the karaoke and cranked up the dance music. The thumping bass reverberated through Jess's whole body, and she needed to have some fun. Jess put her hand on Michael's wrist and shouted over the music, "Dance with me."

When Michael didn't respond right away, Jess leaned closer and inhaled her perfume. Subtle and androgynous. Not unlike Michael herself. Jess glanced at the firm column of Michael's neck. She remembered the trickling sweat she had seen on Thursday night. The skin looked so smooth, so touchable. A rush of heat flowed from where Jess's fingers rested on Michael's hand and made its way all the way to the pit of her stomach. She felt her face flush and she jerked her hand away. *What is going on with you, Jess? Get it together.*

Michael leaned back. "I need another drink first."

"I second that!" Morgan pulled Michael out of the booth and tugged her toward the bar, leaving Stevie and Jess alone.

Jess, disappointed, sat back against the booth and stirred her now melted ice with a straw. It wasn't long before Stevie scooted closer to Jess.

"Are you avoiding me? On my birthday?" Stevie crossed her arms and raised one eyebrow.

"I just didn't want to kill your game." Jess eyed the younger women Stevie had invited, who were currently rubbing up on each other on the dance floor.

"I only have eyes for you, my dear." Stevie took Jess's hand and brushed her lips across her knuckles. The gesture might have been sweet or even sexy coming from someone else, but Jess was tired of Stevie hitting on her. She knew that Stevie had bed partners she considered friends when their clothes were on, and from the flirting and innuendos, Jess gathered Stevie wanted to add her to that list. Jess knew some people, straight and gay, had friends they slept with, but Jess didn't sleep with friends. *Be real. You don't really sleep with anyone.*

The unwanted attention was getting to the point of annoyance. Jess knew one of her biggest flaws was being too nice, but not accepting dates, cutting off hugs before they were too long, and not letting Stevie cuddle up to her at the movies should have been clear signs she wasn't interested. If she was honest with herself, she would have to admit that her discomfort was the primary reason she had begged Michael to come tonight.

"I know you're not interested in me, Jess, but it's my birthday." Stevie stood and held out her hand. "Will you dance with me? Just as friends?"

Jess didn't quite know what to say. No matter how often she had told her, Stevie never seemed to understand or acknowledge that Jess was not interested in her that way. Was she now admitting that she understood there could be no sex in their future? Jess was sure it could be hard for someone as confident and self-assured as Stevie to accept rejection, but maybe she finally had. Jess was skeptical, but Stevie seemed sincere.

"Well, it is your birthday." Jess took her hand and led the way to the dance floor. She rested her arms lightly around Stevie's neck, and Stevie placed her hands on her waist. Jess was pleased to think the two of them might be able to develop a friendship; after all, Stevie really was fun company and a hell of a dancer.

Jess danced up a storm. She was out of breath by the time

a slow number started, and they began to sway to the music. Stevie moved her hands up and down Jess's back and looked into her eyes.

"You know what I'd like for my birthday, Jess?" Stevie's speech was slurred. She brought her hand up to caress Jess's cheek with her fingertips and tightened the hand on her lower back.

A ripple of apprehension grabbed at Jess as she realized Stevie was at it again. Had she not just told Jess she was okay with being friends? Jess didn't want this to go any further. Why did she even agree to dance with Stevie?

"What's that, birthday girl?" Jess tried to sound teasing, but realized her tone sounded much more flirtatious than she had intended.

Stevie lowered her lips and attempted to devour her mouth in a sloppy kiss. Jess pushed on Stevie's chest in an attempt to free herself. She knew that Stevie was pretty drunk, so she was not as offended as she might have been under normal circumstances. And while Stevie could be an egomaniac, she would never in her right mind force herself on anyone.

Stevie backed up, embarrassed. "Shit, I'm sorry. That was so stupid."

"It's just…I mean I don't…" Jess didn't quite know what to say.

"Don't say anything. I am being a drunken ass. And out of line." Stevie seemed genuinely apologetic. She stepped back and shoved her hands in the pockets of her jeans, looking anywhere but at Jess.

"Yeah, it was." Jess punched Stevie on the arm and smirked. "Don't let it happen again."

After some of the awkwardness had worn off, she wished Stevie a happy birthday and went in search of Michael. She was ready to get the hell out of Nine's.

❖

After finishing another beer at the bar, Michael decided she had stayed long enough to satisfy her obligation to Jess. Looking at her bill, she realized she had drunk more than she thought. This fact was even more obvious once she stood up. Yeah, it was definitely time to go. Michael knew how to pace herself, but tonight all she could think about was drinking enough to forget how good Jess looked.

Morgan was talking to a cute gay couple and waved when she realized Michael was about to leave. She waved in return and went in search of Jess to say good night, and to reluctantly wish Stevie a happy birthday.

She rounded the corner of the bar and spotted Stevie and Jess in the corner of the dance floor near the stage. As she got closer, she noticed Stevie's hand wandering down Jess's back. She scolded herself for the surge of jealousy she felt. Jess could dance with whoever she wanted. After all, it was Stevie's birthday. Why wouldn't they be dancing together? They were friends.

Michael held the wooden stair rail and navigated the wide steps to the dance floor. She paused at the bottom step when she noticed Jess's hands were on Stevie's chest, and Stevie's tongue was in Jess's mouth. Michael stood, shell-shocked. Her head began to spin. Had she been wrong? Did Jess have feelings for Stevie? Was this why she wanted Michael and Stevie to get to know each other? Because Jess and Stevie would soon be lovers? *Lovers.* She pictured them rolling around in bed and laughing and making love. Jess throwing her head back in delight as Stevie touched every inch of her body.

Shoving a hand through her hair and taking a deep breath, Michael attempted to become calm. She could not remember the last time she had felt such turmoil; it felt as if she was on fire. Realizing her hands were shaking, Michael turned away. She had to get the sight of them out of her mind. She had to get away from Stevie. She had to get away from Jess. *Now.*

Before she knew it, she was back at the bar, slamming down a ten-dollar bill and getting a double shot from Robin. The burning tequila slipped down her throat, and she placed her shot glass on the table and requested another, ignoring Robin's questioning eyes. She wiped the sweat that had broken out on her forehead. Michael was a private person and did not wear her emotions on her sleeve, but right now, she didn't care. She didn't care about anything but obliterating the sight of them together from her mind. That or obliterating Stevie... she could easily see herself throwing punch after punch. The thought appealed to her more by the second, and she realized she needed to leave the bar before she did something stupid. *Like throwing Stevie through a fucking wall.*

Just as she reached the door she felt a soft hand on her arm.

"Oh, thank God you're ready to leave too." Jess fell into step beside her.

Michael said nothing and slammed her hand against the bar door to push it open.

CHAPTER FOUR

It was near one o'clock, very quiet, and they were the only car on the road. Each time Jess spoke, Michael turned and stared out the window to watch the passing streetlights. Jess knew Michael hadn't wanted to come to the party, but she didn't expect her to be an irritable sourpuss in the passenger seat afterward. After the debacle with Stevie, all Jess wanted to do was spend quality time with Michael, laughing and lounging around as they did most Friday nights, but she feared a carefree, relaxing end to the evening was out of the question.

"What's bothering you? Did something happen tonight?" Jess hoped she wouldn't increase Michael's bad mood by asking about it. She attempted to put aside her annoyance with Stevie and concentrate on being a friend to Michael.

"I don't like the way Stevie treats you," Michael slurred. "Like a piece of fucking meat."

Michael acted protectively with everyone, but as she mentioned Stevie, there was strange anger in her voice. Why bring up Stevie at all? The night was over. Michael had a bad habit of avoiding talking when upset. Jess was not about to relive the Stevie drama so that Michael didn't have to talk about her own unexpressed emotions.

The incident on the dance floor left her uncomfortable,

and she didn't want to think about it anymore. Rather than continue the discussion, Jess said nothing. After several minutes of driving in silence, Jess pulled into Michael's reserved parking spot and turned off the engine. Michael stumbled to the sidewalk. After a night of drinking and spending time with friends, Jess usually said good night to Michael at her building's elevator, then hopped in her car and headed home. Michael's current state made her worry, and she decided to at least help her upstairs. Jess cupped Michael's elbow and guided her to the building. Michael took the keys from Jess and fumbled to find the key to the elevator. Jess could tell they would be standing there all night if she let Michael keep trying. She reached over and slipped the keys from her hand.

Michael leaned against the elevator wall, arms crossed and a scowl on her face. Jess blew out a breath and mirrored Michael's pose, taking a stance on the elevator's opposite side. "What's going on, Michael?"

"I'm fine." Michael stared at the floor and shoved her hands into her pockets. She looked as if she had been caught with cheap beer on her breath, sneaking in after curfew. Jess remembered Michael at sixteen, dealing with the intensity of being a teenager. Her irritation melted away. Morgan had once told Jess that she could read Michael's emotions like no one else could. Could this anger be masking something deeper? Was she hurting? Not knowing what had happened to upset Michael made it hard to know what to say; any comforting words might seem inadequate. Jess hated feeling helpless when someone else was upset. She did the only thing that she thought might help. She wrapped her arms lightly around Michael's neck and embraced her. Jess sighed as she felt Michael relax. She put her head on Jess's shoulder and pulled her closer.

It seemed remarkable to Jess that less than twenty minutes

ago she had been wrapped in Stevie's embrace, one that made her skin crawl, and now in Michael's arms, there was nowhere else she would rather be. She turned and placed a small kiss on Michael's forehead in an attempt to erase the furrows. Michael's skin felt like warm silk. Jess let her lips linger.

A small sound escaped Michael's lips. The sound was so quiet Jess wondered if she'd imagined it. Michael rested her hands on Jess's back, elbows bent and with fingers splayed against her shoulder blades. The soft breathing against her neck stirred a response in Jess, and she wondered if drinking two large cocktails fueled her strong reaction. She released her hold on Michael before she felt driven to do anything more.

When they reached Michael's front door, Jess followed Michael as she stumbled toward the corner of her loft that served as the bedroom. The king-size bed was set low to the floor on a vintage frame, one they had found on one of their many antique store trips. Last spring, they had spent a long weekend refurbishing the old piece of furniture, bringing it back to its intended splendor, and it became one of Jess's favorite things in Michael's loft. The sheets were a dark navy blue with small red squares, and Jess bought them for Michael because they reflected the vintage style of the bed frame. Michael toed off her sneakers and plopped facedown on the large bed with a groan.

"You'll need to drink some water, or you'll regret it in the morning." Jess retrieved a tall glass from the kitchen, held it under the tap, and reflected on the evening. Michael had never before shown interest in her relationship with Stevie; in fact, Michael avoided the subject whenever possible. Why did she now seem so irritated with the way Stevie treated her? Cool water washed over her fingers, and Jess realized she had become lost in thought. She emptied some of the water and returned to Michael's bedside.

Jess set the glass on the night table, sat near Michael on the bed, and played with a loose string on her jeans. "Are you okay?" Jess whispered.

"No," Michael said, the sound muffled because she was facedown.

"Michael," Jess placed a hand on Michael's shoulder, "you know you can tell me anything, right?" Her fingers lightly brushed some strands of hair that had come loose from Michael's short ponytail.

"Not this," Michael said.

What's wrong? She again tried to comfort Michael. She drew small circles on Michael's back with her fingertips, and Michael turned to face her. Her eyes were heavy and tired, yet she looked as though she was about to speak. Michael had never looked so vulnerable. Jess yearned to know what was inside her heart and mind. Jess wanted nothing more than to take her into her arms and make all her worries disappear.

"Let's get you out of these clothes so you can sleep." Jess pulled Michael up and reached for the bottom of her polo shirt. It was soft cotton with large blue stripes, well-worn like most of Michael's wardrobe. Rather than looking old or used, all her non-business clothes just looked comfortable and loved. Jess thought Michael looked great in everything she wore, but she most liked seeing her in casual things.

Michael lifted her arms to allow Jess to remove her shirt. Jess's breath made a sharp intake after she saw the smooth planes of Michael's stomach. She had seen Michael dress and undress many times, but it had never made her flush before. She wondered if Michael did crunches or sit-ups. Michael's stomach was flat and hard, unlike Jess's soft, slightly rounded belly. Maybe Michael got a strong core from all her physical work. In any case, Jess was thankful for a moment to gaze at it. *Knowing* Michael had an incredible physique and *ogling* her incredible physique were two very different things. Jess shut her eyes and continued to pull off the shirt.

Jess tugged, but it was difficult to lift, and she needed to open her eyes. She was greeted with the sight of Michael's breasts encased in a navy sports bra. Her gaze traveled up to the half of Michael's face that she could see. Michael's lips were parted and her breath came in short, shallow bursts. It smelled like alcohol and spearmint, an oddly sexy mix. Jess continued to stare at her mouth, mesmerized, until Michael struggled with the shirt and threw it on the floor.

Jess watched in awe when Michael moved. Her muscles flexed even from the simple act of pulling her shirt over her head. Jess wouldn't have called Michael olive skinned, but she could not find a pale patch anywhere. The skin on Jess's stomach was translucent compared to Michael's, a result of never wearing a two-piece bathing suit. Michael wore a bikini top and board shorts when she swam. Was that how she stayed so tan? How had Jess never noticed it before? *Too much to drink, Jess. Too much to drink.* With difficulty, she tore her gaze away from Michael's chest and looked in her eyes. Her brown eyes, almost black. Michael stared back with a hypnotic intensity. Being that they had been friends for so long, Jess had seen a number of emotions pass across Michael's face: defeat, happiness, grief. This look she did not recognize.

She searched Michael's eyes, trying to figure out what she was thinking and startled when Michael's hand came up to caress her cheek. At first the touch seemed innocent, but Michael leaned forward and began to trace Jess's lower lip with her thumb. Michael swayed toward her, and Jess reminded herself of the fact that Michael was drunk, and she should put an end to this. Yet at the same time, she shivered from an unexpected chill at feeling Michael's touch.

In slow motion, Michael lowered her lips to Jess's. The

first thing she registered was the silky feel of Michael's mouth. Incredibly soft and intoxicating. Their kiss started slow. Agonizingly slow. It felt like warm honey moved inside her veins, and all her limbs turned heavy. Her mind became fuzzy and she could not prevent her body from responding. She rested just her fingertips on Michael's shoulders, afraid of what she might do if her entire palms came to rest on the toned muscles. The tip of Michael's tongue traced her bottom lip, and Jess deepened their kiss. Emboldened by the murmur that escaped from Michael's mouth, she let her hands wander lower. What on earth was she doing? This was Michael. Her best friend. Her buddy.

Her buddy who had a body to die for.

All thoughts flew away and she let her hands run down the perfect stomach she was so distracted by moments ago. She let her short nails drag along the firm muscles in Michael's torso. Michael's lips trailed a wet path down her throat and then back to her mouth. Her fingers touched inside the hem of Jess's T-shirt, but much to Jess's disappointment, they didn't move any higher. Or lower. Jess was ready to jump out of her skin. Heat pooled in her belly and a moan escaped her throat. She couldn't stand it. She had to have more and pushed her palms hard against Michael's shoulders.

Michael pulled her magnificent mouth out of reach and rested her head on Jess's forehead, squeezed her eyes shut. Jess guessed this must be Michael trying to gain back control. Confusion and arousal fought inside Jess as she tried to decide what to do next. Who initiated this? Who was calling the shots? When Michael's eyes opened, the heated look was replaced with one of sadness. Michael peeled one hand away from Jess's body and with the other pulled her down on the bed. Jess went willingly; in this bizarre state she would do anything Michael asked. Jess's eyes closed and she felt Michael's warm hand grasp her fingers and squeeze. She stilled and kept her eyes closed.

Jess vibrated with need, wanted to straddle Michael's thigh and demand her attention. Instead she kept her eyes shut and wished her heart would stop pounding. She felt terrified and exhilarated at the same time. Jess was used to going months without the touch of another, yet even after her longest solitary stints, she had never responded with such an enormous, aching need for another woman.

Opening her eyes, she was crushed to find Michael fast asleep.

She looked beautiful, her dark lashes resting against her cheeks, her chest rising with each even, deep breath. She looked down at their hands. Michael's strong, tan fingers clasped her smaller, delicate ones. The differences were stark. Jess, now even more confused, dropped Michael's hand and crept from the bedroom. She let herself out of the loft and into the elevator.

As she descended to the parking level, Jess felt weak in the knees. What the hell happened? She was in a twilight zone. Stevie had kissed her, which was unwelcome and sloppy. Then out of nowhere she had kissed her best friend. It had taken her breath away. Yes, sometimes friends became lovers, but she never thought that would happen with Michael. They had known each other for too long. It was obvious they were both cemented in the friend zone. She had known that since high school. *Haven't I?*

She knew the kiss with Stevie was a mistake, and it didn't mean anything; Michael's kiss was another story. Michael's kiss was…it was…drunk. *She was drunk, Jess. Don't be stupid.* Surely it didn't mean anything either. It was a silly mistake.

By the time Jess got to her car, she had made up her mind that the evening was an aberration, and it was not going to get in the way of her lifelong friendship with Michael. They could talk about it tomorrow, and no doubt they would both agree their crazy kiss was due to the alcohol, and they would go back to being just friends. Best friends. Years from now they would look back and laugh about it.

Leaning back against the head rest in her car, Jess brought her fingers to her lips and traced their outline…What if she couldn't go back?

❖

Michael awoke to a splitting headache for the second time this week, relieved to find herself in her own apartment. In her own bed. Alone. Turning her head as slowly as she dared, she glanced at the clock. 12:18. *Shit*. A natural early riser, Michael hated to sleep past eight, even when she had been out late. Groaning, she pulled the comforter around her and shut her eyes. As she did, images of Jess filled her thoughts.

It was rare for Michael to drink so much that she was unable to remember the previous night's events. As she attempted to make sense of her jumbled memories, she realized she must have had more than usual. Michael remembered Jess driving her home. Then Jess hugging her in the elevator. The elevator. Yes, she definitely remembered Jess's arms around her. It had taken every ounce of willpower she possessed not to reverse their positions and pin her to the wall. Jess's smell surrounded her even now, hours later.

Jess had stolen her heart long ago. She was gentle, compassionate, and hardworking. She had a view of the world that was pure and positive. Michael envied that. And loved her for it. But more recently, Michael's physical attraction for Jess was becoming something she couldn't avoid.

She had always been attracted to Jess, yet last night was

the first night she'd ever felt close to losing control. Another moment in that elevator with Jess, and Michael would have been kissing her with all the urgency and intensity she could muster.

Stevie. Like a punch to the stomach, Michael recalled the reason she was now nursing such a wretched hangover. Stevie's hands all over Jess, groping her ass. Jess's hands on Stevie's chest. Their tongues intertwined. Michael felt nauseous. Pinching the bridge of her nose, she rolled over onto her back. *How dare Stevie touch Jess that way? How dare she even look at Jess that way. Wait...what if Jess wants it?* What if Michael had been wrong about Jess not returning Stevie's feelings?

Michael had long ago accepted the fact that one day Jess would find someone. Someone she wanted to be with, make a life with. Make love to. However, seeing her with someone was more difficult than knowing it would happen. Why Stevie? Surely Jess had better taste than that! Jess needed someone intelligent, creative, fun, and strong. *You just described yourself, dumbass, and you know she doesn't want you.*

As Michael tried to rid her mind of the unwanted images of last night, she heard the lock turn in the front door. *Jess.* Normally when her friend came over unannounced it wasn't an issue, but in light of Jess's new love interest, she was in no hurry to see her. No, she did not want to see her or that perfect hourglass figure. Michael had never been so thankful for the eight-foot bookshelf used to separate her sleeping area from the rest of the loft. She could hide, jealous coward that she was. Jess rummaged around in the kitchen for only a minute, breezed past the bookshelf, and stopped next to the bed.

"Good morning, sunshine." Jess shook a bottle of aspirin and showed Michael a glass of orange juice. "I figured you might need these."

Michael forced herself to sit. "Thanks."

Jess often spent the night or came over early in the morning on the weekends, but today Michael felt stifled and suffocated with Jess in her space. *Don't be stupid. She's your best friend.* If Jess wanted to spend time with a douchebag like Stevie, well, Michael would just have to bite her tongue. She lifted the glass to her lips and felt the acidic juice slip down her throat and hit her queasy stomach. Opening the aspirin, she shook the bottle until several pills spilled into her palm. She swallowed them at once.

"So," Jess studied her short, red fingernails, "about last night…"

Michael nearly choked. "Yeah, sorry about that." Based on how she was feeling, Michael guessed Jess had to carry her home. She prayed Jess wasn't going to bring up her newfound chemistry with Stevie. Her stomach turned again.

"I mean I was hoping we could talk—"

"Sure. It's just…I'm really late to meet Camille." Michael jumped out of bed and pulled on her jeans and T-shirt. "Some new client. I'll call you later. Okay?" And with that, she hurried from her loft, hoping she could keep the pills down.

CHAPTER FIVE

Michael rushed from the room and left Jess standing alone by the unmade bed. The bed she had tried not to imagine herself in all night. Jess had woken fighting a surprising giddiness. Although she hadn't talked to Michael yet, something about the look in her eyes the previous night told her she felt something too. Although Jess knew she often got ahead of herself when something new and exciting occurred.

After Michael left, she fought back tears as she took the aspirin and orange juice back to the kitchen. Okay, so Michael didn't want to talk. And she apologized. *Sorry about that.* Sorry? Jess wasn't sorry. She was intrigued. And turned on. At least now Jess had her answer. This strong attraction was definitely one-sided. Of course it was. She guessed it was possible that Michael was ashamed for letting it happen. After all, Michael was drunk and confused…that wasn't like Michael. There were few occasions when Michael drank as much as she had last night, and even on those occasions, Michael always took responsibility for her actions. While they were all in the habit of letting go once in a while, Michael was usually the one with the most control, even after a few drinks.

Now that Jess knew Michael wanted to forget the kiss, her

befuddlement increased. Her head pounded as she got into her Passat and headed back to her apartment. Being sentimental and emotional by nature, Jess often put too much stock in events that other people saw as trivial. Maybe Michael wasn't moved by the kiss. Though they didn't discuss sex in detail, Jess knew Michael had her share of willing partners. In fact, women threw themselves at her wherever they went. Michael had probably shared many mind-blowing kisses with other women. Many other women. Beautiful, sophisticated, thin women. Like Camille. Jess felt sick when she pictured Michael's beautiful lips kissing another woman, especially a beautiful former lover like Camille.

The best course of action was to ask someone for advice, as she had absolutely no idea what to do. Pulling into a gas station, she kept the car in drive with her foot on the brake and scrolled through the contacts on her cell. The first few names were of coworkers. Jess loved her coworkers, but she usually kept her private life private. Many people at school did not even know she was a lesbian or were surprised when they found out. After all, Atlanta was still considered the "South," and most of the women she worked with probably stereotyped lesbians as butches in sleeveless flannel shirts, with greasy motor oil under their nails.

Jess came to Morgan's name and pondered. She loved Morgan dearly, but Morgan and Michael were also friends. Jess assumed that since Michael did not want to discuss what happened, she wouldn't want Jess to discuss it with their mutual friends. She put her Passat in park and continued to scroll.

Rebecca, no. Ryan, no. Samantha, no. Sara, hmmm.

Before thinking about it, Jess hit the call button and was connected to her sister's cell. Sara was four years older than Jess, intelligent and successful. She had been an interior designer for seven years, married for five, and a working mother for three. She had practically gone right back to work after delivering Tabitha. Jess envied her drive and accomplishments. She and Jess had little in common, but they were as close as sisters could be.

"Sara Beacon here."

"Hi. It's me," Jess said, nervous that Sara picked up right away. Maybe something was wrong.

"I'm on my way to a lunch meeting. And I don't care how long I've been living in New York. I still can't believe the traffic." Sara muttered something to her cab driver.

As kids they had both hoped to leave Georgia. They were going to be Broadway actresses, or movie stars, or models in Miami. Anything to get away. Georgia didn't hold any special appeal to the sisters growing up. It was dull and boring and it was hard to find adventure. They vowed they would both go on to bigger and better things. Sara stayed true to her word. Two months after graduating from the University of Georgia, she was on her way to fulfilling her dreams in the Big Apple.

Jess visited Sara in New York on a number of occasions prior to graduating from Florida State, and she had quickly realized that for her, those were just childhood daydreams. It turned out she loved Atlanta. It was a great city with rich history and warm weather, and it was affordable. Jess had been living in her own apartment with no roommate for several years, a luxury she couldn't have in a larger city. Teaching afforded her many job opportunities, so why not stay in Atlanta? It provided her with everything a big city had to offer, but satisfied her need to be near open space and beauty of the country. Purple crepe myrtle trees lined her street and a honeysuckle bush bloomed under her living room window. Her place was only a few hours' drive from the beautiful beaches of South Carolina and mountains of Tennessee. Yes, Atlanta was home now.

"Well, other than the horrendous traffic, how are you?"

"Just fine. Busy as usual. Todd forgot to take Tabitha to ballet. Again. I swear if he wasn't so good looking, I'd wonder why I married him. How are you, sweetie? School going okay?"

"I kissed Michael," Jess blurted, unable to hold it in any longer. And saying it out loud made it that much more real. Her palms began to sweat as she waited for her sister's reply.

"You what? What do you mean you kissed Michael? Michael, as in your best friend Michael? The one whose friendship means more to you than anything? That Michael?"

"One and the same." Jess pondered the advertisements for food and cigarettes taped to the concrete walls of the gas station. Jess had never smoked in her life, but in her nervous state, the hot dog for two dollars held some appeal.

"What happened?"

"Last night we went to a party, actually, I begged her to come. We both had some drinks, you know. It was a good time. I drove her home because she had overdone it a little. When I walked her up to her loft...I don't know. It just happened."

"Kisses don't just happen, Jess! Especially not with friends."

Her sister had no idea how often such a thing did happen with lesbian friends. Michael and Jess's friendship spanned the better part of fifteen years, and Sara considered her a second younger sister. There was no way she would let anything get in the way of Jess and Michael's friendship if she could prevent it. Ever the older sister. Maybe this was why Jess had hesitated before dialing Sara's number.

"Sara, I don't know what came over me. One minute I was helping her undress and the next—"

"Why, pray tell, were you helping her undress?" Sara's tone was harsher.

"Come on. We've undressed in front of each other dozens of times. But something different happened. I don't know the word, it was mesmerizing, I guess." Jess gripped the steering wheel as she remembered that smoldering look.

"Well, how was it?"

"I wish I could describe it. Or explain it. It was breathtaking. I've never experienced anything like it. Ever."

Sara was quiet for a moment. "What does Michael say about it?"

"Not much. When I brought it up she avoided the subject and rushed out."

"And what if she had wanted to talk, what would you have said?" Sara's voice was softer now but still had an edge of concern.

"That I…that we…" *That we should kiss again. And often.* She couldn't say it out loud.

"Jess, you have to be realistic about this. She is your best friend. This can't go anywhere. Don't lose her as a friend because you both lost control of your hormones. Let it go."

"No, you're right. I know you're right," Jess said, putting her car in reverse to pull out of her parking space. Sara was right. Their friendship was far too valuable to risk.

After an abrupt good-bye and a promise to call later, Sara hung up, and Jess thought about their conversation for the entire ride to her apartment. Yes, Sara was right.

Then why does letting go feel so wrong?

❖

Although her anger subsided, Michael was in a foul mood all day. After running some errands and going to the gym, she worked on a private project that wasn't for commission. Staying busy worked well, and she thought little about Jess's attempt to discuss her make-out session with Stevie. Later, sitting alone in her loft, sketching and flipping through TV channels, she had time to relive the horrible scene.

Michael felt consumed with the task of accepting Jess's freedom to date. She could not for the life of her figure out why Jess would want to talk to her about Stevie, as only a handful of times they had discussed dating or sex. When in a group they discussed general sexual comments, but nothing specific. During those conversations Michael and Jess both had little to add, letting Morgan and Camille say whatever was on their minds.

There was one exception. The night Jess had come out to her.

For old time's sake, the night before Michael left for the Savannah College of Art and Design, they decided to have a sleepover like they used to in middle school. When they were freshmen, Michael had put an end to the sleepovers, claiming her mom said she needed to concentrate on her studies. Little did Jess know it was because of Michael's difficulties being close to Jess without revealing what was in her heart. There was no way Michael was going to torture herself by sleeping in the same bed with Jess, feeling the warmth radiating from her body, hearing her breathe.

It was a great night, and Michael would remember it forever. They laughed about high school, old friends, and fun times. It was the first time Jess introduced Michael to the Hawaiian Special pizza. They were both on the floor leaning back against the bed, legs stretched out in front of them. Plates and napkins littered the rug, along with yearbooks and other pictures from their years in high school. After finishing what was left of the pizza, Jess grew serious.

"What's wrong?" Michael asked, concerned.

"I have something to tell you. Something I hope you'll be happy to hear," Jess said, twisting a napkin in her hand.

"Okay. What's up?" Michael asked, more calmly than she felt. What could Jess possibly have to tell her?

"I think, I mean I know...I'm a lesbian," Jess said. She looked Michael straight in the eye.

Michael choked on her soda. Jess? A lesbian? At first she was in shock. She had never talked about girls with Jess. That was probably due to the fact that Jess was the only girl that existed in Michael's mind. A lesbian?

"I know it sounds crazy. I kept hoping I would meet a guy that made me feel something. But I feel nothing. And the weird part is that I've never felt anything for a girl either. But I know I could," Jess pleaded. "I hope you can understand. I thought if anyone could, you would be able to." Michael came out their freshman year of high school.

Michael couldn't speak. Her heart soared at the knowledge that no one had ever made Jess feel special, not in the way Michael wanted to make her feel, not in the way she deserved. Her stomach turned to knots just as quickly at the thought of Jess with another woman. She had never pictured Jess with a boy. Jess just wasn't interested in boys. Maybe deep down she knew Jess was also a lesbian, but she hadn't allowed herself to imagine Jess with anyone. Now what? It would be torture to wait around while Jess tried to find the right woman for her. Suddenly, leaving for college was a whole lot more appealing.

"I'm glad you told me," Michael lied, knowing this was an important moment for Jess. She needed Michael's support. Michael hated to admit it, but she would have much rather gone to college with the thought of Jess being asexual. Not with boys, but certainly not with girls.

"I...well...there is something else I want to talk to you

about," Jess said, avoiding Michael's eyes. She blushed. Had she already met someone? Was she going to ask for tips?

Michael swallowed as she nodded, not trusting herself to speak just yet.

Jess hesitated for what felt like hours. Michael prayed she would just spit it out and put her out of her misery. At least she was leaving tomorrow morning, and she would not have to meet this mysterious person.

"I want…I want you to…" Jess began, looking at Michael.

"You want me to what?" Michael asked, more harshly than she had intended.

"I want you to be the first. My first." Jess turned her eyes away again.

It was the most wonderful, horrible thing Michael had ever heard. Jess wanted to be with her? Jess wanted to make love? Michael had imagined their bodies rolling in the sheets for years. Images haunted her. Before she could stop herself, she let her mind run with her fantasy. She pulled Jess up by her hands and ran her hands through her hair. Jess placed her hands on Michael's hips and tilted her head up for a kiss…

Had Jess been harboring the same amorous feelings and emotions for Michael all this time? She could only hope. Michael held her breath as Jess continued.

"I don't trust anyone but you, Michael. You are my best friend. I know you'd never hurt me. I just…I don't know. I thought we could just try it out…practice," Jess said, shyly meeting Michael's eyes.

Michael felt nauseous. *Practice? She wants to practice with me? She doesn't want to make love to me the way I've been dreaming about?* The sick feeling in Michael's stomach turned to anger.

She jumped to her feet and began to pace in front of the closet. "Practice! What do I look like, a fucking call girl? No!

No, we are not going to have sex!" Michael ran a shaky hand through her long hair. As soon as the words left her mouth she knew she had gone too far. Jess turned away from her with embarrassment. Michael cursed under her breath.

"I'm sorry, I just…I'm sorry." Jess began to pick up the trash all over the floor and place it in the empty pizza box.

"No, I'm sorry," Michael pinched the bridge of her nose and ran her hands through her hair again. She knelt down beside Jess, stilling her hands. She tried to control her rising temper. "I didn't mean it to sound that way. It just isn't that easy." Michael paused, knowing her next words would be some of the hardest she would ever have to say. "Sex is important. You will meet someone you trust, someone you care about. And that is something that you will share with them. Not with me," Michael said, pushing a lock of Jess's hair behind her ear. Her heart burned as she spoke every word. While she would love nothing more than to lie naked with Jess and make love to her for hours, she knew Jess didn't love her in the way she needed. She wasn't going to put herself through that only to fall more in love with Jess.

Jess lifted her eyes, tears flowing down her cheeks. "You're the best friend I've ever had." She wrapped Michael in a tight hug.

"Same here." Tears filled Michael's eyes.

Now here Michael sat, still pining after all these years, still mindlessly filling page after page in her sketchbook with drawings and doodles of Jess. Still angered at the thought of Jess with someone else. Still sickened by the idea of Jess giving herself to someone who was nowhere near good enough.

Michael realized it was almost seven, and she had to be over at Camille's in an hour for Girls Night In, a tradition the four friends established when Morgan got her new job at the law firm, and Michael got her first commission. Once a month, they got together, no matter what. A few drinks, fun movies, relaxation with good friends.

Usually Michael looked forward to these evenings, but not tonight. Though she never stayed angry at Jess for long, she still reeled from their morning conversation. Michael couldn't figure out if she didn't want to go because she was still angry at Jess or because she knew the minute she looked into those soft blue eyes, Jess would be forgiven. *Pathetic*.

❖

After countless attempts to concentrate on paperwork, Jess rubbed her eyes and shut down her laptop. It was unlike her not to be able to work. She could always work. Oftentimes she used it as an escape from her personal life or to avoid things that were bothering her. Writing new lessons, finding fun activities for her students, reading new research studies on autism: she knew these things inside and out, and they required little emotional input. She could do them on autopilot. Today nothing distracted her thoughts from Michael and the kiss they'd shared. She replayed it over and over, feeling every touch and every caress again. Amazing. It was surreal, how perfect it was. Yet Michael felt nothing. Or did she?

Jess walked into her bedroom and undressed. As she went about getting ready and putting her makeup on, her mind still raced. Thinking back to the moment right before the kiss, Jess saw something in Michael's eyes. Something she had definitely never seen before. Passion? Desire? Was Michael embarrassed about what happened? Maybe she felt ashamed because she let it happen when she had been drinking. Or maybe she was embarrassed because Jess had never seen her quite that drunk.

It was weird to admit her attraction to Michael, after

all these years of friendship. Thinking back, though, it was obvious. She had just tried hard to hide it from herself. Jess was reminded of one incident in particular. They had been swimming in the lake near Michael's childhood home; they must have been around sixteen. Jess remembered vaguely that Michael had to leave early for some reason or another, so she excused herself to get dressed behind a tree. While Jess went in search of her own tree to change behind she accidentally caught a glimpse of Michael nude. Strong shoulders, small pert breasts, and a perfect butt. A warm feeling overcame her. She thought it was due to embarrassment from seeing Michael naked. It wasn't until she came out that she realized it was arousal. Almost a full minute passed before Jess had moved away from the sight of Michael's nakedness. Steadying herself against a tree trunk to catch her breath, she tried to forget the stark beauty of Michael's body. Jess had never told Michael.

Meeting her eyes in the mirror, Jess wondered if Michael found her attractive. She knew based on comments from Camille and Morgan that Michael had her share of casual encounters. What did Michael look for in a woman? Jess looked down at her large breasts and soft stomach. Turning to view her profile, she rubbed her hands down her sides and back up over her breasts. She supposed she could pass for attractive. But did Michael think so? The way Michael kissed her would indicate she did. The look in Michael's eyes, the feel of Michael's hands in her hair and around her waist, pulling at her. Jess shivered from the memory of it.

"This is insane," Jess said aloud as she looked at herself again. "The hell with it."

If Michael could forget about it, so could she. A romance wouldn't work. They were best friends, and Jess was afraid Michael's taste in women did not extend to the plump schoolmarm type. *Just forget it.* But how? Her body had vibrated with desire twenty-four hours after a kiss that lasted only ten seconds. Yes, they were best friends and had been for years, but the innocence of their friendship was ruined the second Michael's lips touched hers.

CHAPTER SIX

Camille lived in an older home restored with a warm sense of Southern charm, located on Main Street and behind Fairfield Park. The wraparound porch overlooked a large yard with an abundance of pink azalea bushes. With Michael's help, Camille had painted the shutters a robin's egg blue, a bright contrast with the white wicker porch furniture. A narrow hallway led to the old-fashioned kitchen and Camille's office in the back of the house.

"You survived the dreaded birthday party, huh?" Camille asked when she greeted Michael.

"Yeah, I guess," answered Michael, sticking her hands into her worn jean pockets and following Camille to the kitchen.

"Jamie had a gallery opening I couldn't miss. Sorry I couldn't be your support." Jamie was another young artist Camille represented, and Michael had met him at an opening of a new gallery in downtown Atlanta several years ago. With Camille's persistence and sharp business sense, his career was also beginning to take off.

"How was it?" Camille handed Michael a bottle of beer, then started the popcorn.

As the microwave whirled and kernels began to pop, Michael hesitated, not sure she wanted to relive the night enough to explain what she had seen, but she also knew that Camille might understand the way no one else would.

"Somewhat better than slicing my Achilles tendon with an X-Acto knife."

"What happened?"

Michael popped the top off her beer and leaned against the counter. "I was about ready to leave when I saw Stevie and Jess kissing."

Camille stared for several long moments. "No! Aren't they just friends?" she finally asked, stunned.

"Damn right. I thought so too."

"Well, what does Jess say?" Turning her back to Michael, Camille opened the hot bag of popcorn and dumped it in a large bowl. "Did you guys talk?"

"No way in hell will I talk to Jess about her love life. Why would she even think I'd want to hear about it?" Michael pulled several napkins off the table and slammed them next to the popcorn.

"Because she doesn't know she is the love of your life. Or that you worship—"

"The ground she walks on. I know, I know," Michael said with a mocking tone. "But I don't think I can handle her talking about someone else." Michael had tried on numerous occasions to explain the importance of their friendship, but Camille always suggested she tell Jess the truth. Why? So she could be crushed when she found out Jess could never love her that way? *No thanks.* She wasn't about to throw herself at Jess's feet only to have her heart stomped on.

Michael leaned back against the counter and rubbed her forehead. Camille wrapped her in a hug.

"I'm sorry, hon. It must really be getting tough if you're willing to talk to me about it." Camille pulled back. "Do you want to go out with that woman I told you about from work? Carla? She is really sweet *and* has a killer body."

"No, I don't want to go out with anyone." A vision of Ally flashed before her eyes, and she remembered how empty and unfulfilled she felt leaving her hotel room.

Camille clasped Michael's hands. "You can't keep torturing yourself. You need a distraction."

"The only distraction I need is one I can create myself. You have anything new for me?" Michael gave a cocky smile, her usual charming way to change the subject. She did not want a pity date or another hookup. Camille often said it: Michael was incapable of becoming intimate. She could share her body with someone, but her heart was padlocked. Jess owned her and she wasn't about to have a one-night stand with someone *Camille* recommended. After waking up with Ally the other morning, Michael made yet another promise to herself that was the last time she would use another woman as a distraction from Jess. Michael knew she wanted Jess, but she also knew she couldn't be with her. *Damn.* She needed relief bad, and just telling Camille about Stevie made her itch to find another hot woman and lose herself in sex. *Don't do it. Put your mind on work.*

"I actually have a lead, should know something solid by Tuesday," Camille said, as the doorbell rang. She stopped at the kitchen door and turned to Michael, giving her an encouraging look. "We are going to have fun tonight. No worries."

❖

Jess straightened her shirt and fluffed her hair. It wasn't as if this was a first date. First of all, Michael didn't even want to discuss what happened. Secondly, Camille and Morgan would both be here as well. *What was there to be nervous about?*

When the door opened, she dropped her hands in hopes that Camille had not seen her primping. Jess was very fond of Camille, even though she'd had some relationship history with Michael. She was more worldly and sophisticated than Jess, and she had always admired her easy grace and powerful presence. When they first met, Jess had been intimidated by Camille, but after getting to know her Jess found her to be down-to-earth and very sweet.

"Michael's in the kitchen. I guess Morgan is taking her time as usual." Camille headed into the living room with a DVD in her hand. Just the mention of Michael's name sent Jess's heart racing. Jess sat down on the couch in the spot she usually chose when Camille hosted Girls Night In. When Michael rounded the corner with a beer and a huge bowl of popcorn in her hands, Jess's breath caught. *Did she look that good when she left this morning?*

"Hey." Michael gave her a small, shy smile.

"Hey," Jess repeated, her smile broadening.

Michael sat down on the couch next to her, as usual. Jess felt a charge right away.

"How are you?" Michael tucked a loose strand of hair behind her ear and turned to face Jess.

"Fine. I'm fine." Jess wanted to run her fingers through Michael's hair, pull it loose of the short ponytail. Jess was about to suggest they talk for a minute when Morgan burst through the front door.

"I swear we need to do this more often. I look forward to this day every month!" Morgan shrugged off her suit jacket and flung it, along with her briefcase, on the floor before plopping down into an armchair.

"Ha, like you have the time." Camille sat cross-legged on the floor near the television and put *Basic Instinct*, an old favorite, into the player. "Michael's schedule is fixing to get pretty busy too."

"What do you mean? New commission?"

Camille nodded.

"Why didn't you tell us? That's great!" Morgan leaned over to slap Michael on the knee.

"Camille hasn't told me much about it yet."

Camille spoke in her official business voice. "I was going to wait until I heard something more concrete but...I have been doing some networking with the editors of a women's magazine in New York. They are looking for a dramatic piece for their building's entrance." Camille winked at Michael with obvious pride.

Something close to jealousy nipped at Jess. Ridiculous. Of course Camille would be proud of Michael. What if it wasn't just pride? What if Camille had some weird resurgence of her romantic feelings for Michael? Jess shook her head. *Stop freaking out.*

"What magazine?" Morgan asked with excitement.

After sorting through a few of the magazines in a basket, Camille pulled one out with a svelte model on the cover wearing a tiny golden dress.

"*La Femme!*" Morgan squealed as she grabbed the magazine and began flipping through the pages.

"Michael, this is big," Jess said, trying not to look at the glam model too long. Fashion magazines never boosted her body image any.

Michael held out her hand to get the magazine from Morgan. "Have they seen my work?" She turned the pages slowly, glaring as if she had never seen the magazine before. Maybe she hadn't.

Jess leaned in and read aloud some article titles: "'How to Hula Hoop Your Way to Better Abs with a Victoria's Secret Model' and 'Twentysomethings Reveal the Most Awkward Song Ever Played During a Hook Up.'" *Oh, my.*

Jess kept her smile in place as she thought about what this new job would mean. Would Michael need to move? Atlanta wasn't exactly a hotbed of artistic activity.

"I sent them a digital copy of your portfolio. They will want you, Michael. They would be fools not to."

They want you. No, I want you. Jess cringed. Where had that thought come from? A blush crept up her neck to her cheeks, but she could do little to stop it. Jess had not yet allowed herself to imagine being with Michael intimately. She knew once that thought entered her mind there would be little to distract her from the idea. So she was concentrating on the kiss they had shared and only that.

"I haven't even spoken with them yet. I might not want it. Let's not get ahead of ourselves." Michael set the magazine aside and leaned back into the couch.

Although Michael looked aloof, Jess knew she would want the project. Not for the money but for the work. Michael loved to create things for others, to bring their visions to life. Jess remembered when Michael took her first sculpting class in high school. Michael had been successful with any form of art she attempted, but something about sculpting made her come alive. On many days Jess would open her locker and find some trinket that Michael had made for her. Her favorite was the apple Michael had carved for her out of soapstone. It sat on her desk at work and she touched it for good luck. To this day Jess had no idea how Michael knew her locker combination.

❖

They made small talk until Morgan turned out the light, just as Sharon Stone first appeared. Michael prayed *Basic Instinct* would hold her attention. Her hopes were dashed the moment Jess shifted, putting her warm thigh in direct contact with Michael's. It wasn't as if they hadn't ever brushed up against each other while watching a movie, but Michael found it much more difficult than usual to remain composed.

Halfway through the movie she was doing well and able to concentrate on Sharon Stone's legs, and soon she became involved with sketching the actress's thighs. Then Jess shifted again and rested her head on Michael's shoulder, one of those friendly affections they had shared in the past, but Michael shivered when she inhaled Jess's unique scent. Clean and fresh with a hint of something fruity. Raspberry and citrus maybe? Michael stopped sketching and concentrated on twisting the fringe of the throw pillow resting under her arm so she wouldn't do something stupid. Like take Jess's face in her hands and kiss her, right here in front of Morgan and Camille. *Kissing her.*

It hit her. She remembered last night's dream of kissing Jess. Michael had dreamed of being with Jess before but her dreams had always seemed romantic and sweet, such as lying in bed together or riding horseback on the beach during sunset. No sex. No kissing. Last night her dream had been much more intense and intimate. Downright erotic. *Her sweet soft lips and her supple feminine figure.* A wave of heat settled between Michael's legs. She moved her thighs in an attempt to ease the pressure there, but it only made the ache more intense. Michael did not know how much longer she could pretend she wasn't distracted. "I need another beer," she said and scooted to the kitchen.

Michael took her time, even going to the backyard to put her bottle in the recycling bin rather than leaving it by the sink the way Camille always instructed. She pulled another beer from the fridge and leaned against the counter, trying to cool down. Was this how it was going to be now? Her skin on fire every time Jess was around? Not being able to think due to the blood rushing in her ears...and lower?

Michael returned and squeezed as close to the couch arm as she could get. Jess had readjusted and was now leaning against the opposite arm. The movie ended not a moment too soon.

Michael stretched and walked slowly to the hallway. "I think I'm going to call it a night. I'm feeling really tired."

"I'll text you as soon as I hear from the bigwigs in New York," Camille said.

Michael could see the look of concern of her face. It was rare for Michael to be the first one to leave. Camille would often sit with her and talk for hours after the others had gone home.

"Thanks, boss!" Michael said, as she walked down the hallway, relief flowing through her.

Just as she was about to descend the steps, the front door opened.

"Hey, wait up," Jess said, shutting the door behind her.

Michael turned around, leaned against the porch railing. "What's up, Jess?"

"You rushed out this morning and I just...I wanted to make sure you were okay. About last night."

All of Michael's hurt came rushing back. She looked down at her worn sneakers. "Yeah, yeah, I'm fine. No big deal." *I'm only dying inside.*

"Okay. Because, I mean sometimes...with friends... things happen."

Michael's head popped up. Friends? Such as Stevie? Maybe Jess did have sense and didn't want an idiot like Stevie.

Maybe Jess was embarrassed she had kissed Stevie. *Well, that's more like it.* Michael took a chance she was right.

"Yeah, everyone had a lot to drink. Mistakes happen. Right?" She lifted her shoulder in indifference and laughed, hoping it would ease the tension. Jess looked away. A moment passed, and Michael tried not to stare, waiting for some sort of response.

"Definitely. We still on for Memorial Day? I need some time away."

Memorial Day. Our trip. Michael had been so busy with finishing her last commission and trying not to think about Jess naked, she'd forgotten about their annual trip to Dogwood Bluff, their childhood home. They had not meant for it to turn into a tradition, but after the first Memorial Day there six years ago they kept going back. Michael visited her mother several times a year, but Memorial Day was usually the only time Jess came with her. Jess usually spent her holidays with Sara in New York.

"Of course," Michael said, feeling lighter. Jess and Stevie were not together. At least now she could pretend Jess was celibate, which would help her sleep at night. Although her relief didn't change the fact that she would be spending a very long, very friendly weekend with Jess. She could hardly sit through a two-hour movie with her without combusting.

"Should we leave Friday night or Saturday morning?" Jess asked, folding her arms in front of her chest.

"Let's make it Saturday." The less time they spent together, the better. Michael always found the trips to Dogwood Bluff romantic since they were always alone, unless they were with Annabel, Michael's mom.

Jess leaned back against the door frame. "I can't wait."

Michael didn't know if it was the soft porch light on Jess's features or just Jess herself, but she couldn't remember a time when Jess had looked so lovely. Leaning against the door, her dark hair slightly ruffled by the warm breeze and her smooth skin with the slightest hint of makeup. Michael couldn't move, captivated by Jess's beauty. *You have to stop this.* She couldn't even say good-bye to Jess without falling all over herself. How would she ever survive a long weekend?

Michael sped down the Atlanta streets. Driving helped clear her mind, and she was grateful for the twenty-minute drive back to her loft. She sang to the radio and tried not to think about Jess. She tried not to think about how the hell she was going to survive a long weekend with her. Going to her mother's for Memorial Day weekend had always been something she looked forward to. Lately, though, her reaction to Jess was painful. It took willpower to be around her without imagining touching her. Kissing her. And that damned dream. Michael prayed that her dreams wouldn't take another erotic turn as they had last night. She didn't know if she could handle dreaming about Jess that way at night and then being close to her all weekend.

Her friendship with Jess was something she cherished. Michael worried that if she continued down this path of obsession their friendship would change, and not for the better. This weekend could be the perfect opportunity for her to snap out of it. While she did love Jess with all her heart, she needed to move on. She needed to remember Jess was her sweet friend, not the woman she couldn't have.

It was going to be a long, long weekend.

CHAPTER SEVEN

After completing the sculpture for the doctors on Decatur Street, Michael itched for something to do. She had updated her digital portfolio and worked on an oil painting she planned to give her mother for Christmas, but she was still restless. Camille called on Tuesday with no news from *La Femme*. It was now Wednesday, and she felt jittery. Maybe they'd looked over her work and changed their minds. Michael's sculptures didn't exactly scream haute couture, and perhaps they wanted someone more established in the art world, more known outside of Atlanta.

To prepare for the trip to Dogwood Bluff, Michael made a run to the drugstore. She needed a good excuse to get out of the house. She entered Mason's pharmacy, waved to Herman, and grabbed a shopping basket. Herman Mason was a tall, lanky man who Michael guessed was nearing eighty. Michael liked the small-town feel of the family-owned business. Everyone chatted about this or that in Mason's, and it reminded her of a drugstore in Dogwood Bluff.

"Hey, string bean. Storm coming, no doubt about that." Taking his time packing another costumer's purchases, Herman clapped her shoulder with an arthritic hand when she passed the messy checkout counter.

"Rain doesn't bother us Southern ladies." She winked at him and sauntered over to the toothpaste aisle.

The rain and thunderstorms in Georgia this time of year were a sight to behold. The dark cloud cover blanketing the city was almost eerie. Michael loved the humid smell of rain and the distant roar of thunder. Her mother always told her that God was preparing the earth for summer, that plants and flowers needed all the water they could get before the temperatures reached the eighties and nineties. As children she and Jess had always wished for the power to go out when there was a bad storm. Anytime they heard a clap of thunder, they ran and found their flashlights, a game they shared until high school.

Rain often made Michael think of Jess. They had shared a close friendship since the day Michael fought off the older bullies, but Michael knew exactly the moment she fell in love.

It was ninth grade and Jess had begged Michael to walk home with her in the rain rather than take the bus.

"The bus is humid in weather like this. I can't take it. Plus, the rain is so beautiful," Jess said, spreading her arms wide to embrace the raindrops.

It wasn't the first or the last time they walked home in the rain. It was one of Jess's unique habits that Michael came to adore, such as eating her cheeseburgers with a knife and fork. Or the way she softly touched people on the arm or the leg when she spoke to them, making her friends feel listened to and important when they spoke.

The conversation wasn't particularly interesting or important. They were discussing Jess's algebra test.

"I hate algebra. And Mrs. Coleman doesn't like me. She doesn't even want me to do well. I have to pass this class or my GPA will be shot. I won't get into FSU at this rate."

Despite being bright and enjoying her classes, Jess got nervous about grades. "I know you'll do great," Michael said. "You always do great."

Jess stopped and turned to Michael. Raindrops clung to Jess's long eyelashes and soaked her hair until they dripped onto the straps of her book bag. The chilly rain turned her cheeks pink. Michael had never seen anything so beautiful. Jess stood still for a moment, wide-eyed and serious, and leaned over to kiss Michael softly on the cheek.

Without thinking, Michael leaned into the kiss. She had never been kissed before by anyone besides family, not even on the cheek. The kiss melted her heart, but Michael backed away and shoved her hands in her front pockets, surprised by her response and trying to play it cool.

Jess looked embarrassed by her impulse. "Thanks for being such a good friend. You mean so much to me, Michael."

"Don't mention it."

From that day on Michael saw Jess in a new light. She sketched Jess surreptitiously whenever she could. At night Michael sketched from memory, using charcoal and large sketchpads to capture Jess's lyric beauty—the supple, curvy legs; the wide blue eyes; the Cupid's bow shaping her top lip. Thinking back, she realized she was probably always in love but that was the first day she admitted it. She had been hiding it from Jess and everyone except Camille ever since. She knew their friendship was important to Jess. She wasn't about to mess that up.

It seemed to be a trend in the lesbian world to date your friends, be friends with exes, date friends' exes. It was messy and not for her. She hadn't seriously dated anyone since college, and that was fine. Right now her career was the most important thing, and she wanted to give it all her time and energy. Hard work and good friendships were enough. Good friendships like the one she shared with Jess. Michael was not about to let them turn into some sad, lesbian friendship gone haywire.

Michael paid for her items and left Mason's just in time to catch the first sprinkle of rain. Her cell rang as she jogged down the sidewalk to her loft a couple blocks away. The caller ID read "Camille."

"Tell me good news, Camille. Good news only." She stopped at the elevator gate to catch her breath and wipe the rain from her face.

"How much do you love me?" Camille teased.

"Did I get it?"

"You are meeting tomorrow with the three editors of *La Femme* Magazine. In New York, New York, baby!"

"Oh, do I love you. More than you will ever know. I have been climbing the walls. You're the best." Michael leaned against the elevator as it began its slow climb to her loft.

"I've got you scheduled to fly out at six. I know, it's early for a two o'clock meeting, but it was the best deal I could find. I'll send you an email with everything else: hotel, contacts at the magazine, all that good stuff. Are you excited?" Camille asked, sounding very pleased.

"You're sure I'm right for this?" Michael took pride in her work, but this was the big time. How would she fit into a high fashion, fast-paced environment like *La Femme*? Or New York for that matter?

"Michael, you're not some dumb hick from the backwoods. You have a breakthrough vision of powerful women and people need to see it. Don't doubt yourself on this."

Michael thought about what it would mean for her career if the interview went well. A big project for a well-known magazine would be great publicity—not to mention the work would help keep her mind off Jess.

❖

That afternoon, after a lengthy parent-teacher conference, Jess decided to stop by and see Michael on her way home. Being wrapped up in school work, she hadn't spoken with Michael since Girls Night In. That was Sunday, and it was now Wednesday. They rarely went a day without speaking. Michael had sent her a quick text earlier letting her know the interview in New York was confirmed. Jess hoped things would go well. Michael enjoyed working on small-scale projects that she could sell at art shows and local galleries, but when she worked on commissions she was much happier. Jess could tell how amazing it made Michael feel to be able to bring ideas to life and to see her clients' response when she completed her work.

Opening her umbrella and making a run to her car, she decided against calling to tell Michael she was coming over. She feared Michael wouldn't want to see her. Things definitely seemed different between them since they'd kissed. Michael said herself the kiss had been a mistake. She wished Michael had said it was wonderful—that it had tilted her world on its axis and that she was fighting this attraction too. Things *were* different now. At least for Jess. How could she go back, knowing how much passion could flourish between them?

When she arrived at Michael's loft, she felt edgy. Jess began having second thoughts. Maybe it was a bad idea to even consider a physical relationship with Michael. Sara's voice echoed in her head telling her to let it go. Stepping inside the elevator, Jess closed the gate and crossed her arms. She made a deal with herself as the elevator came to a stop. *I will not explore this unless it is mutual.*

When she walked into the loft and saw Michael sitting

at her computer, Jess's determination went out the window. Michael looked stunning, hair damp from a shower and hanging slightly in her face. She wore a tight white tank top, and Jess could tell she wore no bra.

"Hey," she said when she finally found her voice.

"Hey," Michael said, giving a sexy, lopsided grin as she closed her laptop and stood.

Michael wore glasses with stylish thin frames that accented her bone structure, and Jess wondered why she didn't wear them more often. Michael's posture was cool and relaxed, and Jess could smell her soap. Jess inhaled her familiar scent.

"Sorry I haven't called." Michael put her hands in the pockets of her low-slung jeans. The movement revealed a small expanse of smooth, tan skin below her navel. She shuffled a little closer, and Jess met her halfway. "I'm flying out tomorrow."

"All packed?" Jess cringed at her lame attempt at conversation and averted her gaze from Michael's breasts. A warm, tingly feeling rose in her body. "I just wanted to double-check about the trip. Will you be back from New York in time?"

"No worries." Michael held up her hands. "I'll be back Friday night. Leaving Saturday morning still okay?"

"Perfecto," Jess said, keeping her voice even. She had come with the intention of spending some time with Michael, maybe getting some dinner, but she was fast losing control and her pulse was racing. "Well, I just wanted to stop by. I have some paperwork to get done."

"Okay, don't work too hard. I'll pick you up at your place on Saturday. I'll text you when I get up." Michael opened the freight elevator for her. Jess watched as Michael's smooth, muscled arms left bare by her tank top pulled hard to open the heavy gate. Her forearm flexed, showing a sexy contrast of soft skin and hard muscle. Jess swallowed. *Her work. Think about her work.*

"I'm so proud of you, Michael." She stroked Michael's forearm before she could stop herself. She reached up with her other hand and cupped Michael's cheek. "Just wait until those New Yorkers lay eyes on you." Resisting the urge to run her hands through Michael's hair, Jess dropped her hands and wrapped her in a hug. "And your work."

"Thank you," Michael whispered into her hair.

They separated a couple inches but continued to hold each other. Was she holding Michael or was Michael holding her? Jess looked up into Michael's eyes, and she was lost. Those dark brown eyes looked right into her heart.

Her eyes drifted downward and her gaze settled on Michael's lips. It wasn't her eyes she wanted next to Michael's lips. It was her mouth, her whole body. Jess could feel the heat of Michael's breath on her face, and all she could think about was how luscious Michael's mouth felt when they kissed. She could feel Michael's eyes watching her. Did she want this too? In the moment it seemed the most natural thing in the world to lean forward and kiss Michael's lips. So she did. Conscious not to move her hands from Michael's shoulders, Jess leaned forward to press her lips gently and quickly against Michael's. She kept her eyes open to gauge Michael's reaction. Michael's eyes were open too. It lasted only a second, but the firm press of Michael's lips felt just as amazing as she remembered.

Jess's nerves overtook her. *Slow down. You have to slow this down.* Jess stepped away from Michael, shaking a little, and got into the elevator. She put on the most natural smile she could and said again, "I really am so proud of you."

❖

Michael stood without moving for long moments after she heard the elevator stop at the ground floor. *What the hell just happened?* Michael knew Jess and Morgan sometimes kissed each other hello and good-bye, but quick kisses were not something she and Jess had ever shared. Maybe Jess was overcome with pride and wanted to show Michael how excited she was by giving her a sweet peck on the lips. Michael's heart tore at the thought of having to endure a new level of affection from Jess when she could barely control herself around her anymore.

And what on earth had possessed her to hug Jess? Was it because she seemed so happy about the news? Was it because she looked so beautiful in her floral skirt and red cardigan? Her hair was slightly damp, and probably not styled the way Jess would have wanted, but Michael thought she looked beautiful. Was that why she'd hugged Jess? Okay, okay, friends hug. It was not a big deal.

We don't hug like that.

Retrieving her sketchpad from the coffee table, Michael plopped down on the worn sofa. She scolded herself for letting it happen. A friendly hug was one thing...but she had held Jess. Jess was in her arms, and she felt too good to let go. Michael had been unable to tear her eyes away from Jess's face. She had just begun to feel deep stirrings of desire when Jess moved out of her arms. Relief had washed over her. Relief and regret. Regret that she loved Jess. Regret that Jess didn't return her feelings. Regret that she wasn't able to control her emotions or her body's reaction when Jess was around.

It had felt amazing to hold her. Michael reveled in Jess's soft curves and the smell of her, so soft and sweet in her arms. Was that how she would be in bed, receptive and pliable? Or would she be bold and demanding, taking charge and moving Michael's hands where she wanted them? Michael let her head fall back on the couch as her body throbbed. Her hips lifted when she tried to ease the ache in her groin, but any movement of her lower body only heightened her desire.

Damn it.

With a groan, she picked up a red Conti stick. Countless sketchbooks covered Michael's bookshelves because drawing released her stresses and frustrations. Often she would just start sketching, not even aware of the shapes that would take form. Today's encounter with Jess gave an erotic flow and movement to her art that she didn't know she could produce. After several minutes of mindless drawing, Michael looked down to find the curves and valleys of a beautiful nude woman. Jess had no doubt been the inspiration for the sketch, but Michael's hands were still unable to capture the beauty and grace that defined Jess.

CHAPTER EIGHT

The busyness of the airport at such an early hour surprised Michael. She slung her duffel over her shoulder as she pulled her ticket from the back pocket of her favorite, threadbare jeans. Double-checking the gate number, she pushed through the throng of people toward the concourse. It always seemed so funny to her that a place with so many people could feel so lonely and impersonal. Everyone in such a hurry, eyes down, with bored expressions. Even though she knew many people were greeting loved ones or friends, Michael always equated airports with good-byes.

After grabbing a coffee in the terminal, she waited for her flight to begin boarding. Michael sat her bag in the empty chair next to her and stirred her coffee. It was going to be nice to be away from Atlanta, even if just for the day. She rarely got calls from friends when out of town on business; it allowed her more time to reflect and work. Camille would no doubt be calling, and as thankful as Michael was that Camille had made this opportunity possible, she was in no rush to speak with her either. Every time Michael and Camille had spoken in the last three weeks, Camille would bring up Jess…and not just in a "Hey, how is Jess doing" kind of a way, but a "Tell her you love her" kind of a way. Enough. She wished that Camille didn't know her true feelings for Jess, but since she did, the least she could do was respect Michael's decision and stop bringing it up.

The only other person who knew about her unrequited love was her mother, Annabel. Though they had never discussed it openly, Michael suspected her mother knew. Annabel had a way of knowing everything about everyone. When Annabel asked Michael if she was dating anyone, Michael would give her customary reply of being too busy for a relationship. Not long after this, her mother would ask about Jess. How was school going, had they done anything fun lately, or anything else Jess-related? Her mother was also in the habit of pointing out all of Jess's good qualities as often as possible.

"She is such a pretty girl, isn't she, Michael? And she is so good to those little children," Annabel had said last night when Michael called.

"Yes, Mom." Michael rolled her eyes, glad that her mother couldn't see her. In high school that would have earned her a smack on the head and extra yard work.

"She will make some woman very happy one day," her mother continued.

This comment made Michael hurry to get off the phone. She knew it would happen, but she didn't want to think about the fact that the happy woman in Jess's future would be someone else. Michael knew her mother meant well, but she also knew Annabel agreed with Camille. She should be honest with Jess, tell her the truth. *And risk ruining our friendship.* This was something Michael would not, could not do. Michael had seen too many good friendships go to waste on romance. She wasn't about to put their friendship on the line for the slim chance they might actually be compatible as lovers.

Lovers.

Michael could not even fathom what it would be like to

make love to Jess. Until recently, she had never let her mind wander that far into fantasy, but after her most recent dream it was getting harder and harder not to. Michael could imagine touching Jess's skin. Letting her hands roam over Jess's feminine curves to cup her...

A woman's voice came over the loudspeaker to announce Michael's flight was boarding. Relieved she would maybe be distracted from her thoughts long enough to board the plane, Michael grabbed her duffel bag and headed to the gate.

❖

Jess slammed her hand on the snooze button for a fourth time before sitting up and dropping her feet over the side of the bed. She missed the warmth and coziness of her down comforter and Egyptian cotton sheets as soon as she rose. She shuffled into the kitchen of her apartment to start her coffeepot, and her mind wandered to Michael. She glanced at the clock on the microwave. Michael was probably on the plane right now, organizing her sketches and other portfolio work.

When Michael first started sending her portfolio to potential clients, she and Jess would sit for hours with photos spread all over the floor trying to choose which sketches and photos best represented her work. As time went on, Michael became more skilled at assessing her work on her own. Jess always missed those times together. She knew Michael still valued her opinion, but she felt Michael was taking off into a world she knew nothing about. Would she like New York? Would she meet other talented artists? Lesbian artists? Beautiful lesbian artists?

Oh, stop it. It's not like she is moving there. Jess undressed and attempted to drown her worries with a long, hot, soothing shower.

Jess was thrilled about the great things Michael was accomplishing in her career, but she often wondered if Michael would outgrow Atlanta. After all, how far could she go in a medium-sized city? Didn't all artists long for the bright lights where they would be recognized? *La Femme* would certainly get her additional recognition.

The thought saddened her more than anything. On top of feeling sad, it also made Jess feel guilty. How could she possibly be sad about something that meant so much to Michael? Maybe sad wasn't the feeling. Afraid was more like it.

She'll be back. Remember that.

Jess hoped Michael would return, but what was holding her in Atlanta? Michael was talented and accomplished and on her way. Would Jess lose Michael to bigger and better things? Jess could not compete with the glitz and glamour of New York, and she was positive she couldn't compete with the beautiful, high-class lesbians Michael would meet.

❖

New York streets bustled with activity, and Michael loved it immediately. Walking down the crowded streets, she struggled to keep pace. Atlanta was not a small city by any means, but Michael had never seen people going in that many different directions at one time. There was something languorous and friendly about Atlanta; there was nothing leisurely or polite about New York. The skyscrapers, taxi horns, and smoky smells created a dramatic feel—harsh and aggressive. It was exciting to think she could be a part of it, yet leaving Atlanta for long wasn't really in the cards. She loved the South. It was where she grew up and where she wanted to stay.

Pulling a crumpled piece of paper from her pocket, she

focused on the crude map the concierge had drawn. Glancing at her watch yet again, she realized that she was several minutes early. Sighing with relief, she tossed the map in the trash can and crossed the bustling street toward Dyson's Restaurant.

As she neared the entrance, she glanced in the reflective surface of a window. She looked good. Michael had opted for black trousers and a tailored blue shirt, along with black loafers. She let her hair fall around her shoulders, but that meant she continually had to tuck it behind her ears—a habit her mother never liked. Michael clutched her portfolio, a dark brown satchel with her initials engraved into the bottom right corner. It was her favorite present from Jess when Michael had graduated from SCAD, and Michael rubbed the initials with her thumb as she thought of how proud Jess would be if she landed this commission. With that in mind, she headed for the door and grabbed the polished brass handle.

Taking a deep breath and squaring her shoulders, she strode into the restaurant and looked for the back table where one of the editors, Audrey McAllen, said they had reserved seating. As her eyes adjusted to the dim lighting, she noticed a trio of attractive women gathered around a circular booth near the back wall. One of them waved and stood as Michael approached.

"You must be Ms. Shafer," a woman said, taking Michael's hand in a firm but friendly handshake. She was a few inches shorter than Michael but exuded a confidence that Michael found refreshing. "I'm Audrey, we spoke on the phone."

"Wonderful to meet you. And please, call me Michael," she replied in her most professional-sounding voice and hoped her palm wasn't sweating.

Audrey gestured toward the other two women who stood to greet Michael. "This is Deborah Laney, one of our editors."

Michael couldn't help but notice the sleek suits all three

women wore and feared she was underdressed. She didn't own a suit and wondered if the trio would be put off by her androgynous style.

"And this is Marguerite LeBeau. Our editor-in-chief."

Michael was caught off guard by the woman's penetrating stare. Now this woman was intimidating. And attractive. And she knew it.

"Hello, Ms. Shafer." Marguerite grasped Michael's hand. After researching the editor-in-chief, Michael had learned that Marguerite was from France, but she was unprepared for her thick French accent.

"Camille spoke highly of you," Deborah said, as Audrey sat down next to her and signaled to their waiter. "And we are intrigued by your digital portfolio."

"I brought photos as well, if you would like to take a look." Michael slid her portfolio across the table. "And thank you for your interest."

Audrey and Deborah looked through the pictures and commented on her talent and style, but Marguerite's eyes did not leave Michael's face. She was a little surprised to be on the receiving end of a look like that on a business interview, but she did not mind the attention.

"How do you find New York, Ms. Shafer?" Marguerite asked, folding her hands on the tabletop. She wore no jewelry, unlike the other editors whose hands sparkled with rings and bracelets when they had flipped the pages of her portfolio.

"I find it thrilling. I only wish I could stay longer," Michael replied. Apparently this was good news to Marguerite because she raised her eyebrows and nodded.

"Let me get straight to the point, Ms. Shafer," Marguerite said, shaking her head slightly when Deborah slid the leather binder in front of her.

"Please, call me Michael," she said with a lopsided grin, trying to keep the usual flirtatious tone out of her voice.

"Yes, Michael. We want you for this project," Marguerite said with certainty.

"Really? I'll be honest. I was surprised when Camille told me about this. My women are powerful and graceful, but they don't slink around like fashion models. I can't soften the hard edges or the intensity of my work." She hadn't intended to say anything so frank and hoped she hadn't seemed unprofessional.

"Too busy carving to appreciate fashion?" Marguerite's eyes twinkled.

Michael exhaled with relief that Marguerite hadn't been offended by her comment.

"As far as what we want this piece to convey—femininity. Plain and simple," Marguerite continued. "We will give you free rein to create what you want, but the piece needs to convey the female, her grace and her power."

"Power I can do because I don't believe femininity is synonymous with fragility or delicacy. I don't create frail women, but I can provide you strength and boldness." Michael knew honesty might cost her the job; she hoped if that happened, Camille wouldn't kill her.

"Yes, I understand. I will return the courtesy of your honesty and tell you that I am new to *La Femme*, and things are going to change. We are a fashion-forward magazine and will stay as such, but the most important thing about fashion is expressing one's individuality. And that takes confidence. Fearless, beautiful women. That is the new *La Femme*." Marguerite tapped the cover of Michael's portfolio for emphasis. "You see, boldness is exactly what we want."

This was music to Michael's ears. She couldn't care less

about fashion, but she would do anything to bring strength and empowerment to women. She felt an almost an audible shift of the wheels turning in her mind. Work mode took over.

"What mediums are you considering? And have you decided on a completion date?" Michael opened the last page of her sketchpad to take notes.

"Marble," Audrey said, sipping her wine.

"Excellent." Michael resisted the urge to drool. She loved sculpting with marble. The pieces she had previously created were small because it was so expensive.

"We weren't sure if Camille had discussed much about the commission with you. We wanted to make sure our offer was fair: you will have to live in New York to complete the project by the date of the opening of our new office at the end of August. Of course we will pay for your expenses and anything else you require," Deborah said, slipping a small piece of paper across the table with a number on it.

Michael read the six-figure offer and took a gulp of wine to calm her nerves. She tried to comprehend such a large sum of money landing in her bank account.

"It looks like we have a deal," Michael said, allowing her smile to broaden.

❖

Rubbing her tired eyes, Jess decided to shut down her laptop and call it a night. She stretched and shuffled to the bedroom to check her messages. Glancing at her cell, Jess saw a new text from Michael.

"Good news," the text said. Jess's heart began to hammer as she thought of all the things that might change when she heard the news. She pulled on her favorite, worn baseball T-shirt, flopped down on the edge of the bed, and called back.

"I got it. I got the job." Jess could hear the grin in Michael's voice. Having known her for years, Jess wasn't surprised Michael sounded steady, but Jess could still read her emotions. "I'm flying back up in a week to get started. They are putting me up in a hotel for two months. The piece will be too big to move."

"Michael, congratulations! That's wonderful." Jess was happy for Michael, but she felt sick at the thought of her being away for so long. They usually spent more time together during Jess's summer break.

If she visited Sara in New York a few times, though, then she could see Michael some. If Michael wanted to see her, that is. Or had the time. On second thought, that seemed desperate. Jess could survive a summer without Michael. She could go to the movies a lot, and the ones she liked. Michael hated the crowds in movie theaters.

"I will see you tomorrow at eight, right?" Michael asked.

Jess loved how concerned Michael sounded.

After saying their good-byes, she pulled the soft blanket around her shoulders and replayed the conversation. Two months in New York? How was Jess ever supposed to understand her new feelings for Michael if she wasn't even around? And what if she didn't come back? Jess wanted more than anything for Michael to be a creative success and achieve her dreams. To live her life to the fullest. But what if that life didn't include Jess?

❖

After the phone call, Michael tilted her head back and shut her eyes in contentment. She was so glad Jess was in her life. So glad she could share things with her. When something good happened—or something bad, for that matter—Jess was the first person she wanted to talk with. Michael couldn't imagine life without Jess. If that meant keeping their friendship platonic, that was exactly what she would continue to do. No matter how hard it got. She found a tiny bottle of tequila in the hotel mini bar to celebrate.

Feeling resolved to keep her feelings about Jess private, she dialed her mom's number. Annabel also would be thrilled to hear the news. Michael bounced up and paced around the small hotel room as she waited for her mom to answer.

"Well, Michael! What happened at the interview? Do they love you?" Annabel's Southern drawl always seemed stronger when she was excited.

"I don't know about all that, but they definitely love my work. I'll be living in New York while I complete the sculpture. Will you come visit me?" Michael teased.

"You know I will! Oh, Michael, honey, I am so proud of you. So proud." Michael guessed her mother was about to grab the nearest tissue box. Annabel cried when she was happy, sad, excited—she even cried at church. The woman just couldn't hold in her tears.

"Mom, don't cry now. This is good news." Even though she had witnessed her mother cry a million times, it was never something she enjoyed.

"Oh, you know me," Annabel said with a sniffle. "You'll be busier than a moth in a mitten! Don't worry about Memorial Day."

"We're still coming, Mom, and I can't wait. I'm picking Jess up bright and early." Her mother loved when Michael came to visit, but she always seemed worried that Michael would miss out on something if she was stuck in Dogwood Bluff too long.

"And how is my Jessica? Have you confessed your undying love yet?"

Michael's heart sank. *My undying love.* Yes, it was undying. Even after she had convinced herself only moments ago that she could keep these feelings to herself, she knew in her heart what her mother had always known—and would never let her forget.

"Mom! It's not like that." A vision of Jess kissing Stevie invaded her mind; it wouldn't happen again, she knew that, but someday Jess would want someone. "She's my best friend, Mom."

"You know you can be best friends with your partner. No one says you can't. In fact, it's probably not a bad idea."

Michael could tell her mother was smiling. *At least one of us finds humor in this situation.* Annabel only wanted the best for her, but Michael couldn't help getting annoyed when she brought up her unrequited love. It was hard enough to deal with the emotions roiling in her head and heart; it was all the more exhausting to defend her need to keep them private.

"I will call you when we leave, Mom. Get some sleep because I know you will be cooking half the day tomorrow. What's on the menu?" Michael asked, changing the subject.

"Your favorite."

"Chicken pot pie?"

"That's right, sweetie."

"We'll be there in the blink of an eye."

CHAPTER NINE

Hands on her hips, Jess riffled through her open closet and groaned. She had packed the outfits she thought were most flattering on her, but she also wanted to bring something special. Something Michael had never seen. Something to wow her. Jess forced herself to concentrate on the coming weekend and not worry about Michael leaving for New York. Her insides turned to mush every time she remembered the kiss they'd shared, and she hoped, somehow, for a repeat. Sharing an unplanned, drunken make-out session was one thing, but Jess wanted more than anything to share an intimate, passionate encounter. It was getting impossible to ignore Michael's sexiness. How her eyes lit up when she smiled. Or the androgynous, subtle perfume she wore.

"What are you not telling me?" Morgan asked from the bed, flipping through the latest issue of *La Femme.*

Caught off guard and ripped from her thoughts, Jess stumbled over her words. "Hmm…what are you talking about?"

"I've known you for how long? I know when you're keeping something from me. And from that dreamy look in your eyes, it sure isn't anything bad." Morgan closed the magazine, placed it on the table next to Jess's bed, and crossed her arms over her chest. "Is she cute? Tell me everything."

Jess decided to get it over with and tell Morgan. She would get the story out of her sooner or later, and they could talk about it like adults.

As she wondered how to say it, she thought about how Michael reacted both times they had almost discussed it. Was Michael so embarrassed and ashamed that she wanted Jess to hide their kiss from her closest friend? Suddenly Jess felt annoyed. Just because Michael wasn't going to discuss their changing relationship with anyone didn't mean that she couldn't.

Jess picked at the flaking nail polish on her thumbnail and didn't meet Morgan's eyes. "I kissed Michael." When Jess looked up, Morgan was staring at Jess with her mouth open. Jess tugged a sweater from her closet and threw it at Morgan. "Say something."

Morgan still stared, letting the sweater hit her face and fall to her lap. It seemed like years before Morgan replied. "Michael? You kissed her? When? How was it?"

"Friday. After Stevie's party. It was earth-shattering," Jess said, pacing in front of the closet.

Morgan rubbed her face and shook her head, her ever-present high, long ponytail swishing around with the gesture. "Well, shit. What the hell happened?"

Jess relived Friday night and explained the relevant details to Morgan, including the uncomfortable incident with Stevie. "Then she tossed her shirt on the floor and...it just sort of happened. I'm not sure who started it. But I was definitely the more sober one." She flopped down on the bed and sprawled her arms out, looking at Morgan who was still leaning against the headboard. "It was...phenomenal. I've never experienced a kiss that amazing. It was unreal." Letting out a slow breath,

Jess realized how much more real it felt now that she had said it out loud. There really was no turning back.

"So, what...are you guys...like dating now?" Morgan said, trying to hide her laugh with a cough.

"Not even close. She told me it was a mistake." The excitement flowing through Jess was replaced with a sadness she didn't want to feel. A kiss that amazing should only inspire good feelings and not fears that Michael would never want someone like her.

"Well, maybe she is embarrassed? She was really smashed."

"Yeah, maybe. Which is fine. I would be willing to forget the whole thing if...if it hadn't changed everything for me. I can't even control myself now, Morgan. She's electric." Jess again pushed aside her sad feelings to imagine Michael's warm lips and firm body. What would it be like to place her hands on Michael's hard muscles? What would it be like to peel her clothes away and touch every part of Michael with her mouth?

"Well, what the hell are you going to do?"

Jess realized there was only one thing she could do. "I'm going to kiss her again."

❖

When Michael drove up to Jess's apartment building the next morning, she was glad she was wearing sunglasses. She stared as Jess strolled down the brick steps in the sexiest pair of khaki shorts Michael had ever seen. She felt an instant arousal at the sight of Jess's smooth legs in motion. Michael tensed her thighs to relieve the tension.

You're a fucking pig, Shafer. Michael forced herself to pull her eyes from Jess's thighs. She imagined those legs wrapped around her. Her hand running up Jess's calf as Michael thrust her hips into her over and over. Since her erotic dream, she had been unable to stop fantasizing. The plane ride home was particularly difficult. The dim lights led to an intense stream of images, something to do with Michael stripping Jess bare as she stood in front of her and kissed her body from head to toe. *Stop. Just stop it.*

Jess turned around to close the wrought iron gate that separated the small yard from the sidewalk. The khakis were almost short enough to reveal the slight curve of Jess's bottom. *Shorts? Since when do you even think shorts are sexy?* Michael continued to scold herself until Jess opened the passenger door and gave her a silly look.

"Talking to yourself?" Jess climbed into the front seat and tossed her overnight bag in the back. Michael closed her eyes for a moment as Jess's scent wafted into her car.

"Just um…making sure I remembered everything." *Yeah, like the vision of your sexy ass permanently etched into my mind.*

"I'm ready for some time away. How about you?" Jess buckled her seat belt and adjusted the strap over her ample cleavage.

"Yeah, definitely." Michael pulled away from the curb and into the light Saturday-morning traffic. Nothing about Jess's outfit was indecent; it was summery and light, but Michael wished she was wearing more. Not only because the amount of skin was distracting but because anyone could see her. Michael didn't want anyone else but her to see that much of Jess's soft, perfect body.

"Shit." Michael cursed under her breath as she realized how chauvinistic she sounded.

"What did you say?" Jess dug into her purse to retrieve a pack of gum. "Want a piece?"

"Sure." Michael held out her hand, praying to everything

holy that Jess's fingers wouldn't graze hers. "I was going to say that Mom is really excited to see you."

"I'm excited to see her too. I feel like it's been forever. Is she still remodeling?" Jess wrinkled her nose and giggled.

Annabel was a compulsive redecorator. She never felt satisfied with a room for long, and even if she did, she would find another room to tackle. Michael labeled it empty nest syndrome, since the obsession with remodeling began not long after she left for college. Michael had visited as often as her busy school schedule would allow, and every time she did, sure enough there was something different. A room would change color, or the furniture would be different. Annabel had redecorated nearly every room in the house at one time or another. Except Michael's room. She told Michael that was too precious to change.

"I think it's the dining room this time. The walls were red, but she says red dining rooms are a thing of the past," Michael said, using her best Southern belle voice.

"Oh, I adore her." Jess stretched back against the seat, fingertips grazing the roof of the Scout. Michael imagined those fingers running down her belly, unbuckling her belt, and stroking her.

"Tired?" Michael asked, forcing her eyes back to the road. Turning onto Glenwood Avenue, Michael was again thankful that she was wearing sunglasses so Jess wouldn't notice her eyes wandering.

"Yes. Isn't that ridiculous? On weekdays, I would have been up for two and a half hours by now. I swear my body knows to relax when it's Saturday."

Body. *Her body. Those legs. Her thighs. Stop it, Michael!*

Michael cursed when she realized that she had missed the ramp to the interstate that would lead them out of Atlanta. *It's going to be a long, long weekend.*

❖

They arrived in Dogwood Bluff around one thirty, having only stopped for cinnamon rolls at the legendary Nathan's Sweets in Andersonville. The trip was made mostly in silence. Jess loved that she didn't feel pressured to speak. Michael had never been a big talker, and when they were together Jess was relieved to know that Michael would understand her silence. It wasn't awkward, and it wasn't tense. Just quiet.

Although the quiet had been soothing, reading every road sign and billboard to keep from staring at Michael's body was taxing after a while. Once on Briar Road, and passing their old high school, Jess allowed herself to glance over. Michael looked confident: one hand draped over the steering wheel and the other resting on the gearshift. It had never occurred to Jess how sexy Michael looked while driving. There was something so seductive about a woman taking control of a vehicle. Michael took pride in any car she drove, taking good care of it and near caressing the instruments as she drove. Was that what Michael would be like in bed? Gentle and slow, caressing each part of Jess…and taking her time? Or perhaps she would be rough and uninhibited. Taking what she wanted without hesitation. The idea of Michael taking charge sent a chill through Jess, all the way to her scalp.

Back to reading the ads for gas stations and fast food, Jess regained control. Minutes later, lifting her eyes to the bright pink crabapple trees that lined Springs Street, Jess realized they were almost home. *Home…* How inappropriate it would be for Jess to explore any attraction to Michael in her childhood home, but how was she ever going to get through the weekend? Jess closed her eyes and leaned against the window.

As Michael turned down the dirt road that led to Annabel's house, Jess felt more at peace. She loved Atlanta, but there was something calming about Dogwood Bluff. Jess rolled down her window and inhaled the sweet country air, its scent a combination of plowed fields, roadside weeds, and thick summer air. It was hot and humid, but the country air felt like a much-needed balm.

In the distance she could see the house coming into view. As a teenager, Jess often envied Michael's childhood home. It was old, but beautifully maintained, and homey on the inside. Jess had lived in a cramped duplex with her mother and sister and always longed for more space and land. It seemed silly to her now that she had ever felt envious, as she spent as much time in Michael's house as she had in the tiny duplex.

The front of the house was full of large picture windows, and there was a wraparound porch on the first and second floor. Oak leaf hydrangeas lined the porch on both sides of the wide steps, as well as a number of hanging plants and ferns. Wicker furniture crammed the first-floor porch and a large swing hung from old rusty chains. There was also a comfy swing on the second-floor porch near Michael's bedroom, where as teenagers they had spent hours talking and laughing.

Several acres of land surrounded the house, and Southern live oak trees dotted the front and back yards. Annabel's nearest neighbors were over a mile away, which made the house seem even more secluded and peaceful. The house was pale yellow, and the small barn in the back was red with classic white trim. Michael's father had built the barn before he died of a sudden heart attack. Michael had only been a few months old and never talked about her dad.

Jess's favorite thing about Michael's childhood home was the large tire swing hanging from a live oak beside the house. Some of the enormous branches nearly touched the ground, and it took little rope to suspend the swing when she and Michael had put it up in the eighth grade. She spent many afternoons swinging on the tire while Michael leaned against the strong oak trunk, sketching or painting. Jess longed for the picture-book simplicity and ease of those days, swinging in the evening breeze and waiting for the fireflies to tell them when it was time to go inside.

"There's Mom." Michael jumped from the car almost before she had it in park and raced to the porch to greet Annabel. She hugged her mother, picking her up off the ground. Michael had certainly not gotten her height from Annabel, who was shorter than Jess and much slenderer. Jess liked how Annabel wore her hair, clasped at the nape of her neck: the need for a simple and functional hairdo was something Michael inherited from her mother.

"There's my Jessica." Annabel came down the steps and wrapped her in a tight "mom hug."

"Cricket!" Michael yelled as the bloodhound bounded down the steps and nearly knocked her over. "Missed you, boy." Michael swatted at the big goofy dog as he tried to catch her hand. He finally gave up and rolled over on his back at her feet. Michael sat right down in the dirt to pet Cricket's belly.

"Michael, get out of that dirt, or I'll tan your hide. Get the bags. I'm taking Jess into the house for sweet tea," Annabel said, as she grabbed Jess's hand and led her up the steps, where the smell of home-cooked biscuits and apple pie greeted her.

"Jess, tell me, how are your students? How is Sara?" Annabel walked down the long entry hall that led to the kitchen in the rear of the house. Even in the summer, Annabel left the doors open so the interior hallway filled with sunlight.

Jess walked slowly down the hall, allowing Annabel to pass so she could examine the pictures crowding the walls. No matter how many times Jess came to Annabel's home, she couldn't help but look at the memories. So many pictures of Michael, as an infant, then a young child. Annabel had cataloged and photographed most of Michael's childhood. While Michael's bookshelves were stuffed full of old sketchbooks, Annabel's walls held too many pictures to count. Some of them were of Michael and Annabel together, but most were solitary shots of Michael.

Farther down the hallway was Jess's favorite. Michael was about sixteen and had just gotten her driver's license. She leaned against the porch railing in front of the house with her hands in her pockets and wearing a cocky grin. Jess had taken the picture and Annabel asked for a copy. Jess kept the same picture, framed on her desk at work. It captured everything about Michael that Jess cherished. Her confidence, her strength, her beauty.

"Would you like a little lemon, dear?" Annabel called to her from the kitchen.

Jess continued down the hallway. "Yes, thank you."

❖

Jess felt more relaxed than she could remember feeling in weeks. Michael and she walked the grounds with Cricket at their heels and relived old memories. Jess was surprised and happy that her recent sexual thoughts didn't make her feel awkward. Jess felt just as comfortable with Michael as always. Being in Dogwood Bluff made everything seem familiar and natural.

Annabel soon put Michael to work with chores and repairs, as she usually did on the first day of their visits home, and Jess suspected Annabel wanted to keep her busy so Michael didn't hover while she was cooking. Running her kitchen was serious business, and she didn't appreciate interference.

If Michael couldn't sample dinner early, she would wander around looking for something to do anyway.

Jess sat back with Cricket on the second-floor porch swing and watched Michael repair a broken slat on the fence next to the barn. She tried to convince herself she had chosen to sit on the upper porch because of the view of the sunset, but soon her mouth went dry as Michael stood to stretch her back. Grabbing the neck of her T-shirt, Michael pulled it up over her head and slung it over the fence, leaving her in a tight gray tank top. Even at a distance, Jess could see the well-defined muscles of her arms and chest, and the setting sun casting a golden halo on her sweat-dampened skin. Jess never fantasized about cowboys, but in this setting she found herself imagining Michael wearing weathered boots and a cowboy hat…and trying to break a bucking stallion.

"I hope you remind her to stop and smell the roses, dear."

Jess nearly jumped when she realized Annabel was by her side on the porch.

Jess coughed into her hand, attempting to hide her surprise.

Annabel wiped her hands on a dish rag. "You know Michael, always on the go."

"She doesn't stop." Jess forced her eyes higher to observe the orange and red clouds of the sunset. "Such a great view. I love it here, Mrs. Schafer."

"Dinner will be ready shortly."

Chapter Ten

After dinner Michael leaned back in her chair with her fingers laced behind her head. If she had to deny her sexual hunger, at least she could satisfy her appetite for great Southern food. The country fried steak, deviled eggs, and sweet potato casserole had distracted her from the thoughts of Jess that had been occupying her mind for the last week. *Or the last fifteen years.* Although there were times when she didn't think about Jess. After all, she was still able to work and pay her bills, to function in society. It was just when her mind wasn't on something important that it wandered to Jess. Or when she was between activities. Or when she saw something that reminded her of Jess. *Who am I kidding? Pathetic.*

"Thanks for the meal, Mom. It's good to be home."

"Wonderful, as usual." Jess carried her plate to the sink. "I still don't know how you can make such an incredible meal without any recipes, Mrs. Shafer."

Michael found it both odd and endearing that Jess still called her mom Mrs. Shafer. After years of trying to get Jess to call her by her first name, Annabel had finally given up and even began signing her cards and letters to Jess with "Mrs. Shafer."

"Practice makes perfect, my dear. I'm sure you two can manage the cleanup." Annabel left them and waltzed happily out of the kitchen. It had been a rule in their home as long as Michael could remember that the chef never did the dishes. When Michael was about ten years old, Annabel had made a habit of leaving the kitchen as soon as a meal was over.

"You wash, I rinse?" Michael gathered the rest of the plates and headed to the sink.

"Deal," Jess said, filling the sink with water.

They fell into a familiar rhythm of washing and rinsing, as they had done countless times before. Relieved that rinsing dishes was an easy and dull task, Michael relaxed until she watched soapsuds slide down Jess's delicate wrist to her fingertips. Then she imagined Jess bathing in the antique clawfoot tub upstairs.

"Oh, and Michael dear…" Annabel called from the living room.

Nothing like her mother's voice to snap her from an arousing thought. "Yeah, Mom?"

"I'm repainting the guest room, and all the furniture is covered and out of place, so you and Jess will need to stay in your room."

Michael dropped a fork she had been rinsing.

"Okay." *Shit.*

"I put some extra blankets in there. You know how cold it can get."

This could not be happening. She was looking forward to a night alone in her bed where her thoughts could torment her in solitude…and if need be, she could handle things herself.

"Just like old times, huh?" Jess joked, bumping Michael with her hip.

"Yeah, just like old times."

❖

Jess stared at herself in the mirror as she brushed her teeth. She had enjoyed the start of their weekend vacation, she felt relaxed and at home, and she had finally been able to force work from her mind. Everything was going wonderfully... except for the fact that she and Michael would be sharing a room, and a bed, for the weekend. Sure, they had slept in the same bed before many times when they were younger—but that was before...*the kiss.*

Their friendship was forever altered, and Jess knew she wanted to explore the new turn it had taken, but this was not the time. Their short vacation in Dogwood Bluff was supposed to be restful and relaxing. Jess looked forward to this time away all year long, and she knew Michael did too. Michael had been stressed lately, and Jess could tell. She seemed on edge. When they went out with friends, Michael was the last one to arrive and the first one to leave. They were seeing each other less than usual, and Michael seemed withdrawn. Maybe it was *La Femme.* Maybe Michael was trying to hide her nervousness from Jess.

The timing was off, not to mention the setting. If Jess was serious about moving their friendship to a more intimate level, she wanted it to be in a private setting. This was Michael's childhood home, and her mother would be close enough to overhear them in bed.

Stop it, Jess. Just stop it.

Her earlier comment about old times had been an attempt to calm her own nerves at the news that they would be sleeping together. Standing near Michael while doing the dishes, she had noticed a slight increase in her pulse. How was she going to be next to her all night long?

Rinsing her mouth with water, she looked at herself in the mirror one last time. *This is not the time or place for... exploring. Just act natural.* Easier said than done.

Rummaging through her toiletries, Jess found her body lotion. She glanced down at the label: Sensual Cinnamon. Had her subconscious packed that? She should have brought her unscented, ultra-healing lotion. Jess grabbed her nightshirt, glancing at the full-size bed. She slept in a queen-sized one at home and knew that the bed at Michael's loft was a king. Shaking her head in frustration, she pulled open the door and walked from the room, wondering how she was going to survive.

❖

After finishing the dishes, Jess had excused herself to shower and get ready for bed. Thankful for a few moments alone, Michael headed to the den for a drink. Her father had always kept brandy in the den by the fireplace, and after his death, Annabel kept up the tradition. Brandy was not Michael's favorite drink, but tonight it would have to do. After pouring a healthy amount into one of the heavy crystal tumblers, Michael sat in a wingback chair next to the fireplace and leaned back. Cricket left his bed by the doorway to sit at Michael's feet, resting his chin on her knee. His big brown eyes seemed to sense her unrest. Her childhood home was one of the few places where Michael always felt at peace, so the fact that she felt edgy was frustrating. This was supposed to be her fucking vacation.

Could she sleep on the couch in the living room? And how would she explain that to Jess? It wasn't like Annabel would let that fly anyway. She had said they would share Michael's room, and so it would go. Michael knew better than to argue with her mother.

Her thoughts were interrupted when Jess walked into the room in a faded gray FSU T-shirt, threadbare from years of wear. The outline of her nipples was visible through the thin fabric. A pair of pink terrycloth shorts left most of her thighs bare. Michael's eyes moved over Jess's body and stopped to take in her dark brown hair. Michael wondered if it was as soft and silky as it looked. Cricket felt drawn to Jess too and hadn't left her side almost all day. This evening was no exception as he left Michael and trotted over to Jess, hoping for some of her attention.

"Is something bothering you?" Jess plopped down in the matching chair across from Michael's and folded her legs under her.

"No." It was difficult for Michael to form coherent thoughts, let alone speak when all she could think about was Jess's legs. "Just sorry for any inconvenience."

"Oh, come on, sleeping with you isn't an inconvenience." Michael could see Jess hiding a smile behind the curtain of her hair.

Michael gripped her crystal tumbler. Was she imagining the innuendo in that statement? Or the sexiness of the delivery? They often joked around, but never in a sexual manner. Camille said she thought Michael and Jess were the only two lesbians in the world that didn't talk about sex. A stab of jealousy came when she thought of Jess discussing sex with anyone.

Jess picked up one of Annabel's redecorating magazines and began to flip through it. "What about Jacob's Cove tomorrow?"

"Sure."

"Maybe your mom will make some of that amazing chicken salad, and we can go on a picnic."

"Sounds great. I'll ask her. We are running some errands tomorrow, but Mom said to tell you to stay in bed until at least ten. She says you need the rest." Michael was grateful for any distracting conversation.

Jess caught Michael's eyes and smiled again. A stunning smile that showed her top and bottom teeth and lit up her entire face.

After several minutes of companionable silence while Michael counted and recounted the flowers on the rug, the grandfather clock across the room chimed.

"Eleven already. I'm such an old lady, but I can hardly hold my eyes open." Jess stood and stretched her arms over her head.

The action pulled her T-shirt tight over her breasts and revealed a small patch of smooth porcelain skin above the waistband of her shorts. Michael could not help but stare. She stood and took one step closer to Jess. She hadn't intended to stand, but Jess's body called to her in some elemental way. Shoving her hands low into the pockets of her jeans, Michael didn't know what to say. Jess took a step forward too. They were only a foot apart.

Jess reached up and placed her hand on Michael's shoulder over her T-shirt. It was common for Jess to touch people when she talked, but Michael was struck by the intimacy of the gesture. Her skin burned where Jess's thumb caressed the bare skin of her collarbone.

"Are you coming?"

It wouldn't take much…

"I'll be there in a few minutes." Michael glanced at the tumbler. "Just want to finish my drink."

When she heard Jess shut the upstairs door, Michael collapsed back into her chair. *What am I going to do?*

❖

Jess awoke feeling rested for the first time in weeks. Something about being back in Dogwood Bluff always put her body and mind at ease. She rolled over and stretched her arms as she glanced at the clock. It was eleven thirty and she wondered if Michael and Annabel were home yet. As she thought of Michael, she turned her head to the pillow resting next to hers. By nature, she was what her mother called a "messy sleeper," waking up with the sheets in a tangle and pillows everywhere. Had Michael ever come to bed?

Jess had stayed awake as long as she could, waiting for Michael. It was surprising that she had even wanted to be awake when Michael's body slipped between the sheets. It would have been much easier if she were asleep for such a sensuous scene. She was ashamed for even thinking anything sexual while sleeping in Michael's house, but still the thoughts had continued. The last time she had looked at the clock, it was a quarter after midnight.

When she'd entered the den the previous night, and Michael mentioned sleeping together, Jess spat out a provocative comment without thinking. It was unlike her to ever say anything sexual to Michael. Michael had stiffened slightly, and Jess wondered if she had gone too far. In the light of day, she regretted the comment, but last night it had felt good to ruffle Michael's feathers a little.

Forcing herself from the warmth of the sheets, she headed to the bathroom for a long shower. After dressing and drying her hair, she headed downstairs to see if Michael had returned from her errands.

"Hi, Cricket," she said, as he trotted over to her when she entered the kitchen.

Annabel had left a note saying there was a plate waiting in the oven. Jess began salivating as soon as she opened the oven door. Scrambled eggs, thick-cut bacon, homemade biscuits, and sausage links. How on earth had Michael been able to keep her figure all through high school? After pouring some orange juice, she headed to the front porch with Cricket. He bounded down the steps and began rolling around in the sunshine, making grunting noises. Jess sat down on the warm wooden porch steps and breathed deeply as she stared out into the yard. Then she lifted her face to the warm sunlight.

The neighbors' homes were visible, but something about the open expanse of land on all sides of the house made Jess feel like she was miles away from anyone. A glorious feeling. One she didn't get much in the bustle of Atlanta. Picking up her fork, she began to devour her breakfast.

❖

"You're quiet this morning, dear," Annabel said, as she pulled the large truck out of the hardware store parking lot. They had visited Hopper's Hardware to pick up some paint that Annabel had ordered to use on her new garden trellis.

"Just glad to be home," Michael replied.

"Is it my imagination, or did my daughter spend the night in an old wingback chair with an empty brandy glass on the table next to her?"

Michael continued to stare out the window. "I guess I just fell asleep. It's a comfortable chair, Mom."

"Oh, my mistake. I thought maybe it had something to do with Jess sleeping in your bed."

"It's just…I'm not comfortable."

"Darling, I know you think I stuck you two together on purpose, but I didn't. This will always be your home, and I would never want you to feel uncomfortable here."

"Don't sweat it, Mom. This is my problem. I'll work through it."

"What's to work through? I know you're going to say it's not like that, and it's none of my business, but did you ever consider that you and Jess just might be right for each other?" Annabel placed her hand on Michael's arm as she pulled to a stop sign.

"We're not." Michael could hear the bitterness in her voice.

It was close to two o'clock by the time they got home. Annabel went inside to freshen up, and Michael unloaded the paint and potting soil to carry to the backyard. As she rounded the corner of the house, she had to readjust the large bag of soil resting on her shoulder just as her eyes settled on Jess across the yard.

Jess stood leaning on the split rail fence facing the large vacant property behind the house. Her hair blew in the breeze, and she held a small bouquet of wildflowers. She was barefoot, wearing a yellow sundress with small white polka dots. She looked completely relaxed and at home. Because Jess faced the opposite direction, Michael was afforded a brief moment just to appreciate her beauty.

Almost as if Jess sensed her watching, she turned slowly and her face lit up. Michael nodded and resumed her trek to the back of the house. Jess ran over to Michael, with Cricket fast on her heels.

"Hey," she said, stopping right in front of Michael.

Jess looked as beautiful as she had ever seen her. Her cheeks were pink from the sun, and her hair continued to caress her face in the breeze. The sundress left her arms bare, and Michael wanted to touch, or at least sketch, the smooth lines of her shoulders. She couldn't pull her eyes away, let alone support a fifty-pound bag of potting soil, and her knees threatened to give way.

Michael placed the bag of soil next to Annabel's small vegetable garden and rubbed Cricket's warm, floppy ear.

"Did you have a good morning?" Michael asked. While

she had been lost in thought and distracted so far during their mini-vacation, she'd forgotten that this was also time away for Jess, and she wanted her to enjoy it.

"Absolutely. I can't wait to go to the cove. It's a great day for a swim."

"Right. The cove. Mom said she will have the picnic packed soon."

"Will she be coming too?"

Would Jess be disappointed to learn they would be going alone? "No. She's anxious to get some things done around the house."

"Okay, just us. Like old times," Jess joked for the second time since they had arrived.

As Michael watched Jess retreat into the house, she went back to the truck to continue unloading. *Just like old times.* The old times when they would go to Jacob's Cove alone and Michael would revel in Jess's innocence and beauty.

CHAPTER ELEVEN

About an hour later, they headed north in Annabel's blue pickup through the winding roads of Dogwood Bluff. When they were young, Annabel would drive them to the cove early in the summer mornings and come back in the afternoon to pick them up. They stayed all day, swimming, laughing, and sharing dreams for the future. It was a place where the two of them could relax alone together, and Michael cherished the memories and still thought of them often.

"What's got you smiling?" Jess leaned over and poked Michael in the ribs.

"I was thinking about the time we were at the cove, and I told you I was accepted at SCAD. I hadn't even told my mom yet. You were so excited."

"Of course I was. It was your dream," Jess said, looking out the window as Michael turned right on Magnolia Lane.

The road wasn't paved and the ride was bumpy as they drove deeper into the woods. Michael slowed to a stop at the point where they would have to hike for several minutes to get to the falls that flowed into the small lake.

"I can't believe we're are here again," Jess said.

"I wonder if you will think it's changed much." Michael lifted her backpack from the bed of the truck and hefted it onto her shoulders. "Do you remember the way?" She pointed to the faded path next to the truck. They had not been to the cove together in at least six years.

Several minutes later she heard Jess's sharp intake of breath as the small waterfall came into view.

"It's as beautiful as ever." Jess squealed as she picked up speed to run toward the smooth grassy area next to the shore of the lake. The cove was crowded with mature black walnut trees, shading nearly every part of the shore and the water. It was a peaceful area with a cavernous feel because of the pockets of sunshine peeking through the branches.

Michael followed Jess down the bank and unpacked their picnic while Jess took off her sandals and dipped her feet into the cool water. The small waterfall at the head of the lake sparkled and added a soothing sound that Michael found relaxing. The rope swing they had hung from a large branch still swayed back and forth in the breeze. As Michael rolled out an old quilt, Jess began to rummage through the backpack for the items Annabel had packed.

"Well, well, well. What have we here?" Jess asked with a bit of shock in her voice.

Michael looked at the bottle of wine and felt embarrassed by Annabel's gesture. *What was she trying to do? Make this like a date or something?*

"Well, maybe she got it as a gift. She doesn't drink much."

"Was she kind enough to pack a corkscrew?" Jess asked, giggling as she handed Michael the bottle and continued pulling items from the bag.

After the generous amount of food was spread across the quilt, Jess poured white wine into the plastic red cups Annabel had packed. Chicken salad, homemade biscuits, fruit, and even brownies were among the goodies. Michael piled two paper plates high with food and handed one to Jess.

"To being friends for life," Jess said, lifting her red cup in a toast.

"Friends for life," Michael repeated and took a long swallow of wine.

Michael was surprised how easily the conversation flowed during their meal, but then again she had always felt so relaxed here. The wine helped too. It wasn't long before the food was gone and the wine bottle empty. After finishing lunch, she stretched out on her side and propped her head in her hand. Jess sat with her legs crossed, leaning against a walnut tree.

"What do you want in your future, Michael?" Jess asked, moving to face Michael and mirror her position, one delicate, manicured hand resting under her dark hair.

Michael stared for a moment, not sure how Jess expected her to answer.

Jess must have sensed her confusion because she went on. "I've seen you with a few women. But…no one serious. Why not? Why don't you have someone special?"

"Too busy. What about you? Do you see yourself with someone?" The second the words left her mouth, Michael regretted them.

"Yeah. You know, I'd like to meet someone someday." Jess let her hand drop and leaned back as she began to elaborate. "Someone strong and capable. Someone with compassion. Someone fun. And someone who worships the ground I walk on." The last bit was said as Jess jumped up and ran toward the water.

Michael did not respond as Jess scurried away. Why did Jess's words strike a raw nerve in her? Was it because that was the phrase Camille used to describe Michael's feelings for Jess? Or was it because it confirmed the fact that Michael could never give Jess all the things she so deserved? *Well, the worshiping part I know I can handle.*

Jess pulled her yellow dress over her head and dropped it to the ground. She wasn't wearing a bra, so Michael was treated to an exquisite view of the cream-colored skin of her back. As Jess hurried to the water, she pulled her panties down and stepped out of them. Michael turned her eyes away. She had enough haunting images of Jess without the memory of her naked skin to crowd her mind. Michael concentrated on running her finger over the circular quilt stitch on the blanket.

"It feels great! Come on, Michael!" Jess squealed and splashed her arms around in the water. Michael held her breath and looked up, relieved to find the deep water covered Jess's body.

Taking her time to stand, Michael realized there was little she could do to avoid this situation. *Whatever doesn't kill you makes you stronger.*

Michael grabbed the collar of her T-shirt and pulled it over her head. She was not embarrassed to be naked in front of Jess. As a matter of fact, she'd much rather be nude in front of Jess instead of the reverse. She would rather ride the MARTA nude than be this close to Jess's naked body.

Her hands shook as she reached for her belt buckle and removed her jeans. Leaving her briefs and sports bra in place to avoid any more naked skin between them than necessary, she stepped into the water and waded to the middle near where Jess floated, her legs and arms stretched. Maybe this wouldn't be too bad. The water felt great. Maybe if she mentally cataloged her sculpting tools she could maintain some semblance of control.

"Come on over here, Michael. I remember when we couldn't even stand in this part." Jess bobbed in the middle of the small lake and raised her arms above her head. The huge smile indicated how proud she was that she could touch the bottom. The tops of her breasts were exposed and Michael repeated under her breath. *Point chisel. Pneumatic hammer.*

Michael swam toward Jess and realized the water really wasn't as deep as she had thought as a child. Jess dipped below the water, and a moment later her shapely legs pointed upward as she did a handstand. With Jess's head below the water, Michael had the opportunity to openly stare without being caught. Michael had seen, drawn, and sculpted hundreds of legs, but none had ever caused such an instant stab of arousal in her. *Mini stone flat chisel. Rondel chisel. Tooth chisel.*

Jess swam toward her under the water and appeared in front of Michael a few feet away, wiping water from her eyes. Before Michael could think of something to say to break the silence, Jess moved closer. They now stood a foot apart, mostly naked, in the most romantic place Michael could ever imagine.

"Do you think I'm attractive?" Jess asked with a somber look on her face.

The innocent question was startling. Deciding a toned-down version of the truth was best, Michael took a breath and looked away. "Yes…I do."

"Sometimes I feel like I must be missing something. I mean, there have been some women to show interest in me… but not for long. Morgan and Stevie both have overflowing dance cards. And of course, Camille." Jess splayed her hands over the surface of the water and observed the ripples flow and disappear.

Michael felt angry at the thought of anyone making Jess feel anything less than perfect. Her mind flashed back to the creep with the fake Southern drawl who'd hit on Jess at Nine's. What had she wanted from Jess? A night in bed and a good-bye in the morning?

"Jess...you...I mean you have so much to offer. You're smart and fun. Unique, compassionate. And you're terribly sexy," Michael said, trying not to sound breathless. Why the hell did she say that?

Jess's eyes shot to hers and Michael was unable to look away.

"Sexy?" she repeated with a teasing question in her voice.

Michael turned away slightly, but Jess swam back into her field of vision, now even closer than before.

Swallowing hard, she forced a small smile, hoping Jess didn't notice her discomfort. "Yes, sexy."

Jess's lips parted slowly and she let out a small gasp as she looked deeper into Michael's eyes. Something turned off in Michael's brain. Some switch flipped and her body was now responding to Jess's commands. Not realizing she had moved her hands, Michael was surprised to feel the smooth, warm flesh of Jess's hips under her fingertips. Michael allowed her gaze to travel over Jess's face. Her pink lips were moist and plump. Her eyes were dark and heavy, and Michael wondered if that was how they looked after making love. Michael's mouth watered at the thought of Jess coming around her fingers. She wanted to see those eyes darken as she stroked the most sensitive parts of Jess's body. As she began to inch closer to Jess in the water, she paused abruptly. *Friends. We're friends. It's the wine.*

Mustering all the self-control she could, Michael let her gaze drift to their clothes on the shore. "We should be getting back."

The spell was broken.

Michael began to swim back to shore. She glanced back at Jess, who slowly followed. She looked hurt, but Michael could not do anything about it. They would both hurt in the long run if Michael admitted her true feelings. Their friendship wouldn't survive the awkwardness of Jess not feeling the same way. They would crumble.

Michael reached the shore and put her clothes on over her damp skin. The sensation was strange and uncomfortable and almost made her wish they had not come to Dogwood Bluff at all. She pulled her hair back and secured it with a rubber band. Michael avoided looking at Jess as she dressed and began to repack the backpack.

The hike back to the truck and the ride home were made in silence. And it was not their usual companionable silence. On the way back they sat near each other in the old truck, but the only way to describe the ride home was "lonely."

CHAPTER TWELVE

During the drive back, Michael could tell Jess was woozy from the wine they had shared at the cove. Jess leaned against the passenger window and made small groaning sounds through the whole ride and also kept apologizing, which was typical when she drank too much. Michael was glad Jess was cutting loose and enjoying their mini vacation, but Jess's relaxed attitude was getting under Michael's skin and causing her to feel things she usually only allowed herself to feel in private.

Jess stumbled into the house, telling Michael she didn't want Annabel to see her that way. She looked adorable and unsteady walking down the long hall, arms outstretched, fingertips running along the wall.

As Jess got ready for bed, Michael unpacked the food containers and threw away the picnic trash. Pulling her sketchbook from the bottom of the bag, she sat down at the kitchen table to flip through the drawings she had done at the cove. Landscapes had never been her strong suit, and she concentrated mainly on rough ideas for the *La Femme* project and portraits of Jess. She couldn't remember the last time she had felt relaxed enough to sketch for fun instead of for work or an outlet for frustration. Many times when she sketched Jess, especially lately, there was a sensual aspect to her drawings, but looking at Jess the cove, the gentle slope of her shoulders and the ease of her smile, Michael felt a tug at her heart. She remembered the innocence and simplicity of the sketches she used to do of Jess when they were younger.

By the time Michael showered and worked up enough courage to crawl into bed next to Jess, she found her fast asleep. Michael pulled back the covers and sat down as gently as she could. She slowly rested her head on the pillow. It wasn't the most comfortable position, but Michael didn't dare move around too much. The last thing she wanted was for Jess to wake up and start talking to her. Or, God forbid, touching her. Michael could not believe the touching she had allowed, and even initiated at the cove, but that place, their special place, always created an overwhelming sense of rightness and comfort.

After closing her eyes, Jess shifted and murmured, then she rolled over and flopped a warm arm across her waist as she rested her head on Michael's shoulder. It was the most exquisite and painfully wonderful thing Michael had ever experienced. Realizing this might be the only time in her life she would be able to hold Jess closely, Michael tightened her arm around Jess's shoulder. Jess's nearness was like an addictive drug, and Michael could not kick the habit no matter how hard she tried. Michael lifted her hand and stroked Jess's silken hair as she inhaled the scent of sunshine and outdoors and the smell that was so uniquely Jess. Dipping her head, she placed a tender kiss on Jess's forehead.

After what felt like a dog's age, Jess again murmured and shifted in her sleep, moving to the other side of the bed. Michael missed her warmth the moment she moved away but knew it was for the best. Enjoying the feel of Jess in her arms for too long was not a good idea. This insanity had to stop.

Her new opportunity in New York had come not a moment too soon.

Michael turned her head to look at Jess. She faced the window, so Michael was unable to see her face, but her steady breathing told Michael she was still fast asleep. Her heart sank as she stared at the back of Jess's head. She pressed the heels of her hands to her eyes to stop her tears, and she rolled over away from Jess and shut her eyes. Sleep eluded Michael. Finally, near dawn, she got up and went in search of something to occupy her thoughts.

❖

The next morning Jess awoke refreshed and well-rested. Light spilled through the soft lace curtains, casting a warm glow on the room. It must be near noon. Jess was surprised she showed no signs of a hangover, as she had drunk more wine yesterday than she had in months.

Putting her arms above her head, she stretched and yawned, enjoying not having to get up to get ready for work. As she came fully awake, she realized that Michael was not in the bed next to her. Across the room a towel lay draped across a chair. She must have showered and left the house early. It was quiet, and Jess assumed she was alone. She was glad Michael and Annabel would have some time alone together.

In no hurry to get out of bed, Jess pulled the covers under her chin and replayed yesterday's afternoon at the cove. They had talked for hours and reminisced about things they hadn't thought about in years, like the time they had borrowed Annabel's truck to go mudding in the middle of the night one summer in tenth grade. The next day, when Annabel had made them wash the truck inside and out, they could hardly stop laughing. Michael promised Jess it was worth the two weeks of laundry and extra yard work she had received as punishment.

Jess's mind flew to the sight of Michael stripping down to her briefs and sports bra by the shore. The sight was breathtaking and it almost seemed to Jess it was happening in slow motion, as if she was in an erotic lesbian film, the muscles in Michael's arms and stomach bunching as she removed her clothes.

Much to Jess's disappointment, Michael had not shed all of her clothes. Jess knew it would seem strange for her to insist that Michael undress completely, so she bit her tongue. It was a catch-22, since imagining Michael's nude body aroused her almost as much as she was sure the real thing would.

The serene beauty of the cove and the small waterfall helped Jess relax; the wine helped too. Maybe too much. Why on earth was she asking Michael questions about her love life? In truth, she wanted to be certain Michael didn't have an immediate interest in anyone. The last thing she wanted was to put Michael in an awkward situation if she was dating someone. Jess didn't want to think of herself as "the other woman" who stole Michael from some sweet, unsuspecting girl. Jess knew that since they had such a close-knit group of friends, she would know if Michael was seeing someone, even casually. Rationality aside, she couldn't help asking. It did not escape her attention how evasive Michael had been when answering.

A sudden stab of jealousy at the thought of Michael on a romantic, candlelit date drew her from the warmth of the bed. Jess grabbed her toiletries and towel and headed for the bathroom. As she turned to the antique claw-foot tub and began to run the water, she remembered the last part of their conversation before leaving the cove.

Did Michael really find her sexy? Of course, as a friend

she had to say something nice. Even if she didn't think Jess was "sexy," Michael was not the type of person to hurt someone's feelings if it could be avoided. Was she just sparing her feelings? Or did Michael really find her attractive?

Her mind flashed back to the kiss they shared in Michael's loft. The look in her eyes then would suggest she definitely found Jess sexy. But a lot of things seem different when someone drinks as much as Michael had that night. As she felt the water warming under her hand, she decided against a shower and plugged the tub so she could enjoy a hot bath.

Trying to think about the situation as clearly as possible, Jess began to examine the facts as she sank into the tub. The most obvious fact was that she could now admit her attraction to Michael. She could hardly be in the same room with her without a flood of arousal rushing her insides. The next undisputable fact was that she and Michael had kissed. Jess tried not to embellish that fact with words like *earth shattering, mind blowing,* or *miraculous.* Thirdly, Michael had said she found Jess sexy. At this thought Jess's mind began to race. Not pretty, or cute, or nice, which were words she was used to hearing describe her. But *sexy.* What exactly did she mean by sexy? Sexy implied something sexual. Sex. Sex between them? Sex with Michael?

"Ah!" Jess groaned and sank under the water. *What the hell am I doing?*

❖

The last day in Dogwood Bluff passed slowly and leisurely. Michael had spent most of the morning with Annabel in town. They visited Mrs. Simpson at the fabric store because Annabel planned to make a tablecloth for her newly redecorated dining room. She was relieved to return back to the house and have some time to relax before going back to Atlanta. As much relaxation as she could get considering all the thoughts and feelings racing through her.

While Michael had enjoyed their weekend getaway, her nerves were on edge and she was in a borderline state of arousal at all times. Before arriving in Dogwood Bluff, Michael had been nervous about the thought of leaving the comforts of her loft for two months to work in New York, but now she was seeing it as more of a break from the pain of being so close to Jess. Her mind felt totally in control, but her body betrayed her every conviction at the sight of Jess in a sundress. Or standing on her tiptoes to reach something from a cabinet while wearing shorts. Or Jess waking with her hair all messy, as it might look after a night of heated lovemaking.

No.

No, it was definitely time for a break from Atlanta. And Jess.

CHAPTER THIRTEEN

"Thanks for dinner, Mom, the meatloaf was delicious. You should let me cook for you sometime. Give yourself a rest," Michael said, drying the last dish and putting it away. As it was their last night together, Annabel had opted to sit at the kitchen table while Michael and Jess cleaned.

"You're right, Michael. That microwave doesn't get enough use." Annabel smirked as she patted Michael on the shoulder and headed for the den.

After wringing out the sponge and placing it back in the sink, Jess dried her hands on a small towel and began to follow Annabel to the living room so they could all talk before bed.

"I, um, think I'm going to turn in." Michael stood by the table with her hands in her pockets, letting Annabel and Jess precede her into the hallway.

Jess and Annabel both turned to stare. "It's only nine thirty, dear, are you ill?" Annabel's brows knitted in concern as she walked over to Michael and placed her hand on Michael's forehead, feeling for fever.

"I'm fine. Just a little headache. You two sit and talk. Don't worry about me," she replied with a small wink, heading down the hall toward the stairs.

Jess stared after Michael for a moment, missing her. Was

the headache an excuse to get away from Jess? Jess could feel the tension, but she figured it was one-sided. Until now, Michael hadn't seemed to shy away from her or act strange. Michael had also made no attempt to discuss the kiss, and Jess assumed she had forgotten about it. Or at least she wasn't thinking about it. *Or reliving it.*

Jess felt like a thirteen-year-old girl worshipping some celebrity who would never know she existed. But Michael did know she existed. They had existed together all day at the cove, just the two of them. With a warm blanket of sunshine and intimacy surrounding them. What was going through Michael's head?

"Well, come on, sweetie. Let's have girl talk," Annabel said with a slight giggle as she took Jess by the hand. Jess followed her down the long hall, passing the pictures of Michael on the wall. Annabel took a seat in her favorite chair with an array of decorating magazines on the table within easy reach. Jess plopped down on the rug near Cricket, who was wagging his tail on the dog bed. As she stroked his warm, soft ear, he panted and rolled onto his back.

"Tell me, Jess, do you have someone?" Annabel glanced at Jess over the rim of her reading glasses as she picked up a magazine.

Jess was surprised by the question; she figured Annabel had no interest in her romantic life, or lack thereof. "No, I don't."

"Well, you will always have Michael. She loves you so dearly. Always has." Annabel began skimming the pages of a Southern decorating magazine, keeping her tone casual.

Jess smiled. She was glad Annabel understood how important their friendship was. "We are best friends. I don't see that changing any time soon." At this statement, Jess almost sighed out loud. How could she do anything to jeopardize their friendship? Just because of some stupid attraction she couldn't get past? She felt stupid and foolish for going back and forth in her own mind about what she was going to do, when the fact was, she and Michael did share a friendship that could never be replicated. Was she willing to risk that?

"Best friends," Annabel repeated. It wasn't a question. It was more as if she was making sure Jess had chosen the right words. Annabel looked Jess in the eyes for a long moment, and then added, "Yes, you are." The conversation turned to more trivial things like redecorating and what Annabel's next projects would be.

Jess was only half listening. What did Annabel mean by this little conversation? Did Annabel want there to be more between her and Michael? Did Annabel want Michael to settle down? It occurred to Jess that Annabel must have some sort of woman in mind that she would want Michael to end up with. Was Jess anything like that woman?

Following a lengthy conversation about reupholstering living room furniture, Jess bid Annabel good night and headed toward the bedroom. She opened the door and slipped inside, torn between wanting Michael to be awake and wanting her to be dead asleep. Letting her eyes adjust to the darkness, she went to her duffel bag and pulled out her pajamas. After brushing her teeth and securing her hair in a loose bun, Jess shuffled to the bed.

Nervous, she stopped before pulling back the thick quilt. Jess stared at Michael's sleeping form. Was this what it would be like? Joining Michael in bed every night? Would she want Jess to cuddle up to her and hold her while they slept? Would Michael stay up to finish working and join her in bed after she had fallen asleep? Would they sleep nude, wrapped in each other's arms?

Shaking off her nerves and telling herself she needed to

be an adult about this, she fluffed her pillow and pulled back the blanket. Her breath caught and she bit her bottom lip as she caught sight of Michael in her sports bra and basketball shorts. Michael had one arm above her head and the other was resting lightly on top of the blanket at her side. Jess's eyes followed the path of her arm down to the curve of her breasts to her stomach. The darkness in the room cast shadows on the dips and valleys of her muscles and the soft swell of her breasts. Her skin was so smooth and begged to be touched.

A sudden rush of warmth ran through Jess's body and settled between her legs. She had never in her life been this easily, or frequently, aroused. Just one kiss from Michael's perfectly formed mouth and she was a puddle of mush whenever they were in the same room.

Jess couldn't help but notice that Michael used to wear the same thing to sleep in when they were young teenagers. A sports bra and basketball shorts. She recalled looking at Michael's body many times before and wishing she had been as comfortable with her own. Older now and more accepting of her body, she was comfortable with it. But Michael's body was lean and toned with no imperfections that she could notice. Hard and flat where her own was round with soft curves. Jess eased herself down on the bed. She sat on her knees facing Michael for a moment, just staring.

Would she wake up if I touch her?

Jess extended her hand toward Michael's stomach. As her fingers began to shake, she pulled back. Looking at Michael's skin again, she nearly broke down. Her emotions were all over the place. *I just have to touch her. Just this once.* Jess slowly extended her hand again and drew in a deep, steadying breath. Letting her fingertips rest on Michael's skin, she glanced at Michael's face to make sure she wasn't stirring. Jess continued to caress Michael's abdominal muscles with a feather-light touch, afraid she might wake her. What on Earth would she say if Michael did wake up? *I was just caressing you in your sleep and hoped you wouldn't notice!*

Jess again looked up at Michael's sleeping face and saw no signs of her waking up. Flattening her palm, she laid it flat on Michael's stomach. Breathing in through her nose and out through her mouth, she tried to calm her racing heart. If only she could move her hand higher and cup Michael's breast. If only she could wake her with kisses and make love to her all night the way she wanted to. The way she realized she had always wanted to make love to her.

The comprehension of her true feelings for Michael washed over her like a bucket of ice water. *I've always been in love with her. Always.*

Jess snatched her hand away and scooted off the bed, facing away from Michael. She rubbed her hands over her face and through her hair as she fought a queasy feeling rising in her throat. It all made perfect sense. Why Jess never wanted to hear about the women Michael was involved with. Why she rarely dated, and when she did, she compared each woman to Michael. Why her friendship with Michael was the most important thing in her life.

A feeling of foolishness and naivety came over her. She had been in love with Michael all this time and never even realized it. All these years she spent waiting for the right person to come along, when the right person had been Michael. Wonderful memories of Michael began rushing through her mind. Staring at Michael's eyes as she sketched her portrait more times that she could count, sleeping next to Michael as a young teen when they had sleepovers, Michael always being there for her no matter what she needed. Jess felt ill.

Michael didn't feel this way about her. She would not even acknowledge that something as innocent as a kiss had transpired between them. Michael didn't want her, she could have anyone. Women constantly hit on Michael. She was kind, beautiful, strong. Everything a woman would want in a partner. Everything Jess wanted in a partner. What did Jess have to offer someone like Michael? She was about to leave for New York to complete a commission that would most likely launch her career.

"And I'm just a lonely school teacher," Jess whispered to herself in a half-joking tone. She sank onto the bed without looking at Michael. Jess had been kidding herself about this attraction to Michael. Deep down she always knew that their friendship would change as Michael's success as an artist grew. She wanted nothing more than to see Michael live her dreams of becoming a successful sculptor, even if it did affect their friendship, but she hadn't thought she would lose the love of her life in the process. There was no way Michael returned her feelings, and there was no way a relationship was in their future.

❖

"Michael, I don't know how you wear jeans in this weather. It's hot as blue blazes out here!" Annabel complained as she sat down in a rocking chair next to Michael and handed her a glass of sweet tea. The glass had already begun to sweat in the warm morning air, and Michael drew shapes with her finger in the condensation. She had woken up early and packed her things, then left the house for a long walk. By the time she returned to the house around ten o'clock she needed another shower and had convinced herself the long walk was to work off the food her mother had been cooking the whole weekend and not to avoid Jess.

"I always wear jeans, Mom. It's not that hot." Michael felt

a drop of sweat run down the back of her neck and she pulled at the collar of her worn baseball shirt.

"You little mule. You've always been this stubborn. I remember potty-training you. You would hide your panties in the couch cushions because you didn't like wearing underwear. Doesn't matter if it's somethin' you don't want to do, or somethin' you don't want to accept. You just dig your heels in." Annabel spoke with a harsh tone, but her eyes were smiling.

Michael eyed her mother with a scowl. She wished everyone would just let it go. Things with Jess were at a near boiling point, and she couldn't bear even indirect references to their tense relationship. Her own thoughts had tormented her enough this weekend.

Last night, Michael had gone to bed early hoping to be asleep by the time Jess joined her. She had fallen asleep, but she could not escape Jess. She had dreamt of her all night. Her kiss and her touch. Even her smell. These dreams were becoming more and more vivid. At one point Michael swore she could feel Jess's tongue swiping at the shell of her ear. Jumping out of the rocking chair, Michael grabbed her duffel and took it to the car. Jess hadn't woken up yet, but she was anxious to get on the road.

Michael would be leaving early tomorrow morning for New York to begin work on her commission. She needed a clear head. She needed to put Jess as far from her mind as possible. Maybe this time apart would help.

With a creak of the screen door, Michael watched as Jess descended the front porch steps and put her sunglasses on. Yeah, all she needed was some time apart to forget about her smile, her chestnut brown hair, her beautiful shapely legs.

"Shit." Michael ground her teeth as the telltale tingle of arousal began.

"What Michael, dear?" Annabel asked, bringing over a brown paper bag full of leftovers and more carbs than Michael was prepared to consume after this weekend.

"I'm going to miss you," Michael said, taking the bag from Annabel and putting it behind the driver's seat. She turned and wrapped her arms around her mother's slender shoulders and rested her chin on Annabel's head.

"I am so proud of you dear. So proud. You will do well in New York."

"Thanks, Mom. I love you."

Michael really wished she could see Annabel more often. Maybe if things worked out in New York, Michael could buy a little house in Atlanta. She would even love for Annabel to live with her, but even before she was finished with the thought, she knew Annabel wouldn't go for it. This was her home. Michael knew it would take a lot of convincing to make her leave this place.

"Good-bye, Mrs. Shafer. Thanks for a lovely stay. You will have to come visit me while Michael is in New York," Jess said, approaching the car.

"Oh, I will dear. I know you will be lonely without her." Annabel wrapped Jess in a tight hug, and Jess laid her head on Annabel's shoulder.

Michael could not read Jess's expression because of the dark glasses she wore, but she could have sworn she saw a light flush on her cheeks.

Just your wishful imagination, Michael thought grumpily as she sat down in the driver's seat and buckled her seat belt. After the incident at the cove, Michael had analyzed Jess's every move. Was Jess feeling an attraction too?

Michael tried not to notice the swell of Jess's breasts tight against her T-shirt as she bent to sit in the passenger seat. She also tried not to notice her perfect legs or the way the pink polka dots on her skirt accentuated her pale skin tone, but as hard as she tried, it was impossible to ignore the sight of Jess's body as she got comfortable and clicked her seat belt into place. Michael looked straight ahead and turned the key, waiting for the ignition to purr.

"Ready?" Michael asked.

"Sure thing."

CHAPTER FOURTEEN

The trip back to Atlanta was less than five hours, but Michael felt as if she'd driven the length of the entire Mason-Dixon Line. Jess stared out the window, which she had done for most of the ride, with her bare feet propped up on the dashboard. Her soft cotton skirt left her legs bare from mid-thigh down, and Michael tried to get a glimpse of Jess's skin without turning her head. At one point when Jess dozed off, Michael did stare and was jolted by the shaking of the steering wheel when she drove over the rumble stripe before righting the car. How had she never noticed Jess had a cute freckle above her left ankle?

Traffic was sparse and Michael was able to stay in one lane at a steady speed, so she draped her hand on top of the shifter. The weekend was over. Should she be relieved? Jess would return home, Michael would fly to New York, where the only woman she wanted to interact with was made of marble. Yet somehow, the closer they got to the exit for Jess's apartment, the more depressed she became. The weekend had been magical. Just the two of them, as if it was years ago. Except the near catastrophic fuck-up. What if she had kissed Jess at the cove? Based on some of the interactions they had over the weekend—the flirtatious banter, the near kiss, sleeping in the same bed—Michael wondered what Jess's response would have been if she *had* kissed her, and that was a dangerous line of thinking.

Michael knew Jess to be an incredibly open person. People knew how she felt about them, good or bad. If Jess was harboring amorous feelings for Michael, she'd know it. She knew Jess didn't love her, but was she hot for her? The idea of Jess wanting her made her wet.

Michael had done most of the talking during the ride. Actually, Jess hadn't said much of anything. Was something bothering her? Maybe she was just bummed about heading back to the grind. Michael glanced at Jess and tried to read her expression. The large Jackie O–style sunglasses hid her eyes. Jess turned and the corner of her full mouth quirked up in a half smile. Yeah, something was up. Jess didn't do anything by halves. Not even smiles.

"Can we head to your place? I'm not ready for reality," Jess said, facing the window as she spoke.

The idea of prolonging their weekend twisted Michael's gut. Time with Jess was always something she craved, but after the closeness and intimacy of this weekend, she also needed some time to cool off and collect her thoughts. Michael knew she would have to agree. She would do anything Jess requested.

"Sure, I have some sketches for *La Femme* I wanted to show you." As soon as the words left her mouth, Michael realized how lame they sounded. It was partly true, but mostly Michael wanted to seem unaffected by Jess's request. She continued straight to the next exit toward her loft. Because her voice sounded strained, Michael cleared her throat. She concentrated on the broken white line of the road to keep from thinking about the blood rushing through her.

In the elevator headed up to her loft, Jess remained quiet and distant. This silence felt awkward, and Michael didn't want their perfect weekend to end on a sour note. She didn't want Jess to be upset. If something was bothering her, Michael wanted to know. Michael needed to be a good friend to Jess, even if it meant prolonging her own discomfort and sexual frustration for a while longer.

The elevator lurched to a stop and Michael stepped over to the door and pulled it open, letting Jess into the hallway. Deciding to be up front with Jess, Michael blurted, "Is everything okay?" as she stepped into the darkened loft. She had left a small table lamp on in the living area, but it did not provide much light to maneuver by.

Jess didn't respond, so Michael turned to look at her after she shut and locked the door. Jess looked adorable and sexy at the same time in a faded, threadbare Blondie T-shirt and that damn polka dot skirt. Her hands crossed under her breasts and her head titled to the side as if she were studying Michael from behind the sunglasses she still wore. "Is everything okay?" Michael repeated.

"No," Jess murmured. Michael's heart ached at the pain in that small voice. She dropped her duffel and in two steps was in front of Jess. She raised both her hands to remove Jess's sunglasses. The look in Jess's eyes stole her breath. Michael had been with many women, and had kissed more than that, but never had she seen a look of such unguarded, unafraid longing.

The sunglasses clattered to the floor as Jess backed Michael up to the nearest wall. Michael's back met the rough brick just as Jess's soft hands came to rest on the sides of her face. Michael looked away, unable to meet her eyes.

"What—"

Jess put a finger on Michael's lips. "Shh," Jess whispered and traced the outline of Michael's bottom lip with her fingertip.

What is Jess doing?

Chancing a glance at Jess's face, Michael's eyes were drawn to Jess's moist mouth.

Those lips. That tongue. This woman. This was the last straw. Years of pent-up sexual desire and obsession rushed through her like floodwaters from a dam.

Michael twisted until their positions reversed and she reached up to pin Jess's hands above her head. With deliberate slowness, Michael trailed her other hand down the line of Jess's ribs to rest at her waist. Michael paused for a moment and focused hard on Jess's eyes, searching for some reason to stop. Jess's eyes bored into her, and she saw nothing there but complete arousal and abandon. Knowing Jess wanted this, wanted her, even the second burning of Atlanta wouldn't be enough to stop her from taking Jess now.

When their lips touched, Michael felt as though she had been shoved into some far off corner of the universe. The nearest other living thing billions of light years away. Nothing mattered. Not time. Not control. Not restraint. The silence was deafening and gravity nonexistent.

The adolescent fantasies that followed her into adulthood were insignificant compared to the feel of Jess's pliant and responsive mouth beneath her own lips. With her wrists still bound above her head by Michael's larger hand, Jess leaned into the kiss but allowed Michael to set the pace. This fact did not escape Michael's attention and she trembled at the thought of being in control, of dominating Jess.

Michael was taken aback by the flood of arousal she felt as Jess yielded to her hands and the firm press of her mouth. Squeezing Jess's wrists and trapping her body against the wall, Michael grabbed Jess's chin with the other hand and pushed her face upward, exposing her neck. At Jess's sharp cry of pleasure, Michael bit down hard, not caring if she left a mark. Jess began to fight to free her wrists, which only made Michael hold them tighter. The feeling of overpowering Jess, of controlling her arousal and her desire, was causing primal urges in Michael's body she was unfamiliar with. With her free hand, Michael roughly palmed Jess's ass, pulling her more firmly against her own body. She wanted to throw Jess over her shoulder and carry her to the bed. She wanted to make Jess beg for her touch and deny her pleasure until Michael saw fit to deliver.

As she continued to press her lips into Jess, she grew bolder and slid her tongue inside. Jess opened to her with a small moan, and Michael's knees buckled at the gentle swipe of Jess's tongue. Michael reluctantly let go so she could feel Jess's hands on her skin. Jess seemed tentative but not shy in her exploration of Michael's neck and shoulders. Slipping a thigh between Jess's legs, Michael was rewarded with another small moan as Jess ran her hands inside the collar of her baseball T-shirt.

Jess's mouth was hot and hungry. She tasted like spearmint and summer. In the back of her mind, behind the haze of arousal and throbbing of her body, Michael felt the catharsis of this moment. Every word she had ever read by Shakespeare or Sappho made complete sense to her. If the world swallowed her up right now, she would be happy in heaven with the memory of Jess's lips.

Michael continued her assault on Jess's mouth and she could sense Jess's growing irritation at the barrier of clothing between them. Michael tugged at the hem of Jess's worn T-shirt and pulled it up over her head. Once her shirt fell to the floor, Jess turned her face up to Michael's in search of her mouth.

Before she could kiss her again, Michael kept her mouth just out of Jess's reach, feeling her warm breath caress her face and their lower bodies fusing together. Letting her eyes drift down Jess's face, then to her neck, and then to her round, high breasts in a pink lace bra, Michael's mouth went dry.

"What are we doing?" she asked, breathing hard and trying to control her building emotions.

Jess looked deep into Michael's eyes and once again reversed their positions. Grabbing the nape of Michael's neck, Jess put her lips to her ear and whispered, "Everything."

The remaining self-control Michael possessed crashed down around her as she crushed her mouth to Jess's. The gentleness she equated with Jess was gone, and Michael resisted the urge to cry out as Jess tugged at Michael's bottom lip with her teeth. Michael pushed her tongue into Jess's mouth, nipped and licked her lips as she thrust her hands into Jess's silky hair.

Jess held on tight to Michael's waist, fisting her shirt in her hands, as if she thought Michael would disappear.

Pushing away from the wall, Michael backed Jess toward the corner of her loft that served as the bedroom. With no window coverings, the panes of the large windows cast a grid pattern of ambient street light on the large antique bed. Jess pulled and tugged at Michael's shirt and jeans. Her hands roamed underneath Michael's T-shirt, grazing the bottom sides of her breasts. Michael hissed and grabbed Jess's hands to still her movements; her breasts were incredibly sensitive, and if she wanted to make this last, she needed to slow things down.

Michael backed up slowly. Jess groaned at the loss of contact, but sat on the edge of the bed to observe Michael. As Jess watched, Michael grabbed the collar of her own T-shirt and pulled it off to reveal her black sports bra. Michael moved her hands to her belt and pulled it free, never taking her eyes off Jess's. She released the button of her jeans and pulled the zipper down. Dropping her pants and briefs at the same time, she saw Jess's eyes nearly fully dilate. Michael's chest rose and fell rapidly as she watched Jess's eyes feast on her nearly naked body. Showing her body to Jess she could handle. This she was used to. But her heart was another story.

Finally, Jess's eyes rose to her face and she stood. Michael breathed deeply, trying to calm the tremor in her body and the blood rushing in her ears—determined to hide her desperation. Continuing to look her in the eye, Jess reached behind her hips to the clasp of her skirt. The only sound Michael could hear was the clink of the zipper and her heart pounding. Michael swallowed hard. With an agonizing slowness, Jess pulled down the skirt zipper and pushed the material down her thighs, leaving her pink panties in place.

Nearly whimpering out loud, Michael took in the sight of Jess's body. Her narrow waist gave way to rounded hips, and Michael itched have those milky smooth thighs wrapped around her. Jess's body reminded her of a Renaissance painting—unblemished porcelain skin, round and full in all the right places. This was the first time Michael had allowed herself to appreciate Jess's beauty without constantly keeping her sexual arousal at bay. Michael let the feeling flow through her body. Travel through her. Consume her.

Words she knew she couldn't utter threatened to spill from her lips. She wanted to tell Jess she knew how sweet she would taste. How warm and soft she would be. She wanted to tell Jess her fantasies could never live up to the reality of touching Jess and claiming her, but she knew she couldn't say any of those things. Whatever this was…whatever was happening… she still felt the need to keep her heart hidden.

Michael watched the gentle rise and fall of Jess's chest and realized it wasn't nearly as erratic as her own. While she drew comfort from this, there was still something in the back of her mind telling her this should not be happening. Before

Michael could reconsider the path they were headed down, Jess slowly unclasped her bra. She slipped the straps off her shoulders but held it to her chest a moment longer. Michael closed her eyes, overcome with emotion at the thought of Jess naked in front of her, offering herself for the taking. When she opened her eyes Jess let the garment fall to the floor. Her breasts were round and full, with soft pink nipples begging to be touched.

Michael then reached for her own bra and pulled it over her head. As her breasts were revealed, Jess ran her hand down her belly to cup her own sex. Michael nearly lost consciousness. Michael grabbed Jess's wrist, pulling it away from her body.

"The only person touching you tonight," Michael nipped at Jess's chin, "is me." Her voice sounded harsh, but she couldn't help it. Jess's sexy smile in response let something loose inside her. Grabbing Jess's hands she held them behind her back with one hand and she trailed her index finger down Jess's neck, between her breasts and stomach to rest just inside the fabric of her panties. Jess's sexy smile vanished and gave way to a sensual yet pained expression. *That's better.*

"Understood?" Michael tugged gently on her bound hands until Jess met her eyes.

"Yes."

"Good girl. Now hold still," Michael warned.

Not knowing what else to do, Michael leaned down to kneel in front of Jess as if to worship her. She placed a kiss on Jess's lower belly, just above the line of her panties. Wrapping her arms around Jess's lower body, she continued to kiss the soft skin there.

"Michael."

The sound of Jess's voice as she whispered Michael's name was arresting. Michael had heard her name spoken thousands of times, but now with Jess's warm skin under her fingers, she felt as though Jess was speaking some unknown, romantic language—the word unfamiliar and provocative. She wanted to hear it again. Forever. Not allowing herself to think about tomorrow, she concentrated on that sweet, sexy whisper. Michael was determined to hear her name from those lips again and again before the night was over.

"Michael, come up here," Jess said, pulling at Michael's biceps.

"No," Michael replied firmly with a predatory grin and lifted Jess's hips closer to her face.

Jess brought her hands up to tuck her hair behind her ears, returning Michael's grin and then placing her hand in front of her mouth to hide her giggle.

Staring at Jess's panties, Michael ran her index finger just inside the elastic, and Jess moaned as her head fell back. She placed one last kiss on top of the smooth fabric, then rose to stand in front of Jess.

Michael's smile faded as she registered that this was the first time in her life that she was going to genuinely make love to someone. She put her fingers to Jess's cheek. *God, I love this woman.*

Jess lifted her face to Michael's mouth. Their kisses had lost the urgency from moments ago, but Michael still felt as though she was going to explode. Jess pulled Michael tight against her as they tumbled onto the low bed. Jess ran her hands up and down Michael's back and settled them firmly on her ass as Michael held herself up with locked elbows. Michael thrust her hips forward in a weak attempt to ease the ache that had begun to overtake her center.

Wanting to make it last, but desperate for more contact, Michael lowered her upper body onto Jess. She held her breath at the first touch of Jess's erect nipples against her chest. The feel of Jess's breasts pressed against her own was like a hot brand on her skin.

Sliding her trembling hand down Jess's abdomen, Michael reveled in the feel of her smooth warm skin. Though this was the first time Michael had ever felt Jess's skin in a sexual way, it was as if their bodies knew how to speak to each other. Everywhere Michael placed her fingers, Jess's skin seemed to warm and come to life. Gooseflesh spread over the skin on Jess's arms, and she moaned as Michael attempted to caress every inch of her.

Jess returned the favor wholeheartedly. Her hands moved in a frenzy, pulling at Michael's hair, squeezing her shoulders, and rubbing her back. Jess's fingernails raked across Michael's shoulders as Michael slid her hand all the way down Jess's stomach. All of Michael's muscles bunched as she held herself back. While she had given herself over to this, she was not yet at full speed. Michael feared the intensity and ferocity of her actions might scare Jess. Her hand stilled just inside Jess's panties.

"I won't break. Just do it. I want you inside me." Jess tilted her hips to emphasize her need.

Michael groaned as she palmed Jess's sex and was rewarded with a loud moan as Jess arched her back and squeezed Michael's wrist. Wanting to savor this moment, she spread Jess open. Michael rubbed her finger up and down the length of Jess's sex slowly.

"So hot. So wet. Jess, I could drown in you," Michael whispered.

As she slipped her index finger into Jess's moist heat, she cried out with the joy of it. Michael felt completed. She felt like she was coming home for the first time. Inhaling deeply to try and keep her composure, she opened her eyes to look at Jess's face: eyes closed, lips slightly parted, a fine sheen of sweat on her neck and shoulders. Michael felt Jess push down toward her hand, and she slipped a second finger inside.

Jess continued to run her hands up and down Michael's back, thrashing her head from side to side. Michael's sensory system was on overload, and she felt as if her entire body was about to burst. She straddled Jess's thigh and pressed herself against the firm muscle of Jess's leg. She must have noticed the heat of Michael's sex pressed against her because Jess grabbed a fistful of Michael's hair and screamed out as she pumped hard against Michael's hand.

Knowing she needed to make this last, but not knowing how long she could stand the torture, Michael moved against Jess's leg. The movement began to alleviate the painful throb in her groin while still keeping her primed. It was not her pleasure she was worried about. Michael wanted to make Jess understand how beautiful and how precious she was, and she wasn't going to stop until Jess begged.

Jess's inner muscles gripped at Michael's fingers and she grew incredibly still and rigid. Michael glanced at her face and saw a pained expression as she gave herself over to ecstasy.

"Yes, please. Michael," she yelled as she came.

Michael slowed her own movements to enjoy the sight before her. Jess flung her left arm over her face, and in the dim light Michael could make out Jess's teeth slightly pulling at her bottom lip. Jess looked sexy and sated, pleased and exhausted. As Jess's heart rate began to calm and her grip on Michael loosened, Michael was overcome with the urge to taste her.

"Jess…I need my mouth on you," Michael begged in a shaky voice.

Moving down Jess's body, she caressed her breasts and her stomach, opening her palms as wide as she could. She wanted to catalog every curve, every dip and plain. Michael feared any sculpture she might try to create would be an incredible disappointment after seeing the true beauty Jess possessed.

As Michael reached her destination, she peeled away the last bit of clothing hiding Jess from her view and tossed the panties behind her. She inhaled Jess's scent and almost came without any physical contact. Dipping her finger inside Jess, Michael spread Jess's juices over her folds and up to her clit. Jess arched her back again and ground her luscious hips into the mattress.

Michael's mouth watered as she lowered her mouth, looking up at Jess. They locked eyes at the first touch of Michael's tongue on her. Slowly moving her tongue up and down Jess's sex, she could not turn her eyes away. This was the woman who made her feel whole. She felt more determined than ever to make this something Jess would always remember. Michael wanted to show her that no one had ever really made love to her before. Or ever would again. Michael shut her eyes and put her all into giving pleasure to the woman who gave her life meaning.

Jess began to pump her hips harder into Michael and grabbed fistfuls of the sheet. Jess threw her head back and screamed in a loud, uninhibited cry. She locked her thighs around Michael's head. Michael came undone as she felt Jess's muscles tighten around her tongue.

Michael wanted to slow down, and she wanted to give Jess time to recover, but she had to answer the call of her own body and her own heart. Confessing a deep secret after years of silence, her body shook. She moved up the bed and pressed her crotch into Jess. She felt the throbbing in Jess's center as she began to thrust against Jess's hips. They fit together perfectly. Michael shuddered at the warmth spreading through her. Jess writhed beneath her and slipped her hand between their moving bodies. Jess cupped Michael and her head fell forward to rest on Jess's shoulder as she stopped moving altogether.

"Don't hold back, Michael. Kiss me." Jess attacked her mouth as she slipped her fingers inside Michael. Every muscle in her body threatened to give way as Jess claimed her mouth and her body.

Michael knew her face was slack, mouth hanging open. She didn't care. "Harder," she commanded on a sharp exhale.

With that, Jess flipped her over, never taking her fingers out. Jess straddled Michael's thighs, sitting up, one hand working Michael and the other grabbing her own breast. Forcing her eyes to stay open, she watched as Jess pulled and caressed her own nipple. Michael slapped Jess's hand away and grabbed as much of her large breast as she could fit in her hand. That and the movement of Jess's breasts as she pumped her hand sent Michael over the edge. She shot up and grabbed Jess's shoulders as a powerful orgasm crashed through her body. Her legs shook as wave after wave of pleasure avalanched through her entire body.

A moment later Michael collapsed on the side of the bed, pulling Jess with her. "Good God." Michael nuzzled her face into Jess's neck.

"Michael. Was that…real?" Jess's words were punctuated with soft breaths and moans. She ran her fingers up and down Michael's sweat-dampened stomach in slow circles as both of their heart rates slowed.

"Let's do it again just to make sure." Michael grinned as she moved to capture Jess's nipple between her lips.

❖

Hours later, after Jess had fallen asleep, Michael sat naked at the window across from the bed. Crumpled papers scattered on the floor all around her. Her hands cramped after countless attempts to sketch Jess's sleeping form. No lines were perfect enough, no stroke gentle enough. Setting aside her sketchbook, Michael ran her hands through her hair and relived the most intense experience of her life. This was beyond sex. This was even beyond making love. This was a life-changing, all-consuming, soul-searing event that she never thought she would be fortunate enough to experience. It had outshined any fantasies or dreams. Making love to Jess, touching her body, capturing her at last was something that Michael knew had changed her forever.

Michael pulled on her briefs and wandered to the kitchen in search of something to drink. What had this experience meant for Jess? Michael knew Jess loved her as a friend, but what had changed? Could they have suddenly wandered off the track of their friendship and ended up in fuck-buddy territory? Avoiding details of Jess's love life was an active habit of Michael's, so she couldn't speculate on her sexual habits. Forgoing beer, Michael opened the freezer and pulled out the vodka she kept on hand. Had Jess slept with *friends* at FSU? Had Stevie slept with Jess the night of the party? What about Morgan? Images of Stevie kissing Jess, and then Morgan kissing Jess invaded her mind.

Trying not to break the shot glass, Michael swallowed two shots before capping the bottle. She was trembling again, but not from pleasure. Imaging Jess being as uninhibited and responsive to anyone else's touch filled her with rage. If she thought Jess would sleep through it, she'd throw the vodka bottle across the room, but instead returned it to the freezer.

Michael took pride in being self-aware. She knew she was hardheaded and stubborn, she knew she could be standoffish, and she lately knew she'd been drinking too much. Along with this self-awareness came self-preservation. Things had been unraveling before her eyes the past few weeks and tonight they had come to a head. After tonight, Michael could not fathom the crushing blow that was coming when Jess realized this was a mistake—when she realized Michael could never measure up. Surviving that was something Michael knew would be impossible.

Chapter Fifteen

Before her eyes even opened, Jess smiled and stretched. Her smile widened as she registered her sore and well sexed muscles. The sun shining on her bare skin told her it must be nearing nine o'clock. Sliding her arm to the other side of the bed, she was surprised to find it empty and cold. She rubbed sleep from her eyes and glanced around the space for Michael. *Michael.* The events of last night came rushing back, and Jess felt her body respond.

Jess had slept with a few girlfriends before, and even a near stranger once, but she had never experienced anything like making love with Michael. The connection she felt with Michael last night was intense and palpable. The look in her eyes and the urgency of her movements. While she had been fantasizing about Michael since that first kiss, nothing could have prepared her for their fiery passion and explosive lovemaking.

As Jess stretched her arms and yawned, the sheet fell exposing her tender breasts. A blush crept up her neck as she noticed marks and love bites on her chest. Jess recalled Michael waking her up in the middle of the night as her tongue made its way down Jess's body. Jess had been beyond exhaustion, but something about the frantic movement of Michael's hands and her heated skin made her forget about her tiredness and immediately respond to Michael's mouth. Jess had never come more than once with a lover, and she had never been so relentlessly pleasured by someone. She had read about these kinds of things in magazines and books, yet never experienced anything like that in her own life. It had been a while since she had been with someone intimately, but she knew there was more to it than just her recent bout of abstinence.

Flopping back on the pillow and squeezing her eyes shut tight, Jess tried to relive every feeling, sensation, and touch that she could. Michael was more passionate than Jess could have hoped or even imagined. It was almost as if she was obsessed with bringing Jess pleasure. And by the sound of Michael's moans and the urgent thrust of her hips, Jess could tell that her own desire and release was driving Michael mad.

As much as she didn't want to consider it, Jess wondered if Michael had experiences like this often. Jess had never thought of Michael with another woman, and in light of last night, she really didn't want to start visualizing that now. Could it be that Michael was that passionate and responsive with everyone? Jess had no doubt in her mind that all Michael's women were probably as responsive to Michael's touch as she had been. How could they not be?

Pulling the sheet up to cover her breasts, Jess moaned as the light fabric caressed her sensitive nipples. She smiled to herself and squeezed her thighs together as she was overcome with a sudden wave of arousal. Michael's hands had been calloused from working with tools and stone. The rough strength of Michael's hands as she squeezed and rubbed Jess's flesh had been almost enough to send her over the edge. Jess remembered shutting her eyes tight, praying for the ability to make it last. To draw it out. The culminating event of years, of never letting herself fully realize how she truly felt about Michael.

For the first time she thought about what this meant for their friendship. What did it mean for them? She wondered what last night had meant to Michael and how she would react now that the morning was here. When Michael wouldn't discuss the kiss they shared, Jess was hurt. But this was much more than a kiss, and Jess would force Michael to tell her how she truly felt. Jess was relieved she had taken the Tuesday and Wednesday after Memorial Day off, even though it was frowned upon by her principal. They would have a lot to talk about before Michael left for New York.

New York!

Jess reached over to the low bedside table grabbing her cell phone as disappointment gripped her, replacing the pleasant arousal from only a moment ago. 9:21. Michael's flight left at eight thirty. Glancing toward the closet she didn't see Michael's bags anywhere. Why would she leave without saying good-bye? After everything that happened last night? Jumping out of the bed, Jess wrapped the sheet around herself and wandered out of the bedroom.

"Michael?" Jess said as she rounded the corner to the kitchen, the sheet trailing on the floor behind her. The thought of having to wait two months until she could be naked with Michael again made her whine out loud. Maybe Michael would invite her up to New York for a long weekend? Or longer? Her summer vacation would start soon. Of course Jess didn't want to distract Michael from her work, but how could they be apart that long, knowing how explosive things were?

Jess suppressed a goofy grin when she saw the sketch and folded note on the counter. *Who knew Michael was such a romantic?* Securing the sheet more tightly around her, Jess concentrated on taking in the details, delicately tracing the lines of the drawing with her finger. It appeared to be a charcoal sketch of her, which surprised Jess because Michael didn't use it often. The lines of her face were serene with sleep, and wisps of her hair hung over her eyes. Her lips were heavily shaded making them look plumper than usual, probably due to all the kissing and biting. She looked satisfied and loved. She looked beautiful. Was this how Michael saw her? Still smiling, Jess set the sketch aside and picked up the note. Glancing at the two words written in Michael's handwriting, Jess was befuddled.

I'm sorry.

Wait…sorry? Sorry for what? *Oh, my God. She regrets it.*

Jess's stomach threatened to empty. Here she was, dressed in a sheet in Michael's apartment, by herself, after the most amazing and life affirming event in her life. Why did this keep happening? Why did she keep allowing herself to imagine a deep-rooted romantic connection with Michael, when in truth she was just being a naive idealist? *Who falls in love with their best friend and expects those feelings to be returned?* Could she have misread everything? Maybe Michael wasn't in love with her, but she never would have imagined Michael could make love like that and then disregard everything in the light of day. Jess was almost as angry with herself as she was with Michael.

Shoving the drawing and note to the floor, Jess got dressed in a hurry and stormed out, hoping her anger would eclipse the heartbreak she knew would follow.

❖

Everything seemed to be happening in some sort of hazy slow motion. Michael didn't remember arriving at the airport or boarding the plane. As the seat belt light chimed, Michael turned and looked out the small window. The skyline of New York City held no luster for Michael as the plane made its descent to the JFK airport. Michael stared straight ahead as the woman next to her leaned over to take pictures of the big city coming into view.

"I'm so excited! Have you been to New York before?" The woman seemed like a lovely person, but Michael couldn't help feeling annoyed as she shook her head. She didn't want to talk. She didn't want to breathe. "Have you ever seen anything so beautiful?" The woman sighed as she leaned back to tighten her seat belt. Regret and longing twisted Michael's insides as she thought of Jess, tangled in sheets, one bare leg exposed. Michael had slowly, and quietly, gotten ready to leave that morning. Jess's ivory skin glowed next to the dark fabric of her sheets and Michael itched to sketch her again before making her cowardly exit. She half hoped Jess would wake up and beg Michael to take her again before she had to go. But she hadn't. And Michael knew it was for the best.

She didn't know what had come over Jess last night, but she knew in the morning, Jess would have time to think about her actions. Time to think about Michael's actions and what they meant for them and for their friendship. She knew Jess didn't love her, and it took everything Michael had in her not to declare her love for Jess over and over as they made love. Thank God she at least saved herself that embarrassment. Like in her art, she let her hands do the talking. Michael had been naked and in pain from the pleasure of touching Jess everywhere and it was so much better than any sculpture, painting, or sketch. She could not bear to hear Jess utter the word "mistake" or some variation to describe the night they had shared. So she ran. It was for the best.

The bump and rumble of the less-than-perfect landing only increased her sour mood. Usually after a night of sex, even mediocre sex, Michael was happy, focused and productive. This morning, after sex that had elevated her to a spiritual orbit, she could hardly go a minute without grinding her teeth. Hoping to avoid any further chatter from her cheery neighbor, Michael stared out the window as the plane slowed.

How could she have been so stupid? So selfish? She had succumbed to her outrageous sexual needs and ruined the best thing in her entire life. Now that the situation had presented itself, it made sense to Michael why she had never been able to even consider a sexual relationship with Jess. Michael would never be able to be near Jess again. Not after last night. Not after knowing what her lips and her skin felt like; not after knowing what she sounded like as she came, screaming Michael's name and trembling. Not after feeling her from the inside.

It was over. And now Michael was ruined. How could she ever move on from this? How could she continue her life without Jess in it? Not to mention that fact that sex with anyone else was out of the question. The mere thought repulsed her.

Instead of heading to the hotel, Michael had the taxi driver take her directly to the *La Femme* office building where she would be completing her commissioned work. As she hopped out and handed the driver a few bills, she took a deep breath trying to put everything from her mind, except her work. It wasn't customary for Michael to complete a work in the building where it would be displayed, but it cut costs for the client. And Michael was always hesitant to move her larger pieces anyway.

Before entering *La Femme*'s headquarters, Michael took a moment to appreciate the architecture of the twenty-story building while dodging pedestrians. While it wasn't the largest building on the street, or even close to it, the shiny, mirrored glass exterior reflected the midday sun, and Michael was struck with the beauty of the structure. It looked out of place, since most of the neighboring buildings were stone, or brick, and quite a bit older. A doorman with a round belly and a pressed uniform smiled as Michael approached, and he held the door for her and bowed slightly.

The inside of the building was just as chaotic as the street outside. There were construction workers, painters, and people in hard hats everywhere. The smells of plaster and fresh paint hit Michael as soon as the door closed behind her. Renovation was an understatement. It appeared the entire first level had been gutted and was undergoing a major facelift. There were no walls, only studs and support beams. A large, wide staircase in the center of the lobby looked to be the only thing staying the same, and Michael could see why. It reminded her of a staircase she'd see in a plantation house in Atlanta. It didn't quite match the exterior of the building but it was Michael's favorite part.

She headed over to a tall counter that resembled something that would be at a hotel check-in desk, the only furniture in the space. There was a short man behind the counter playing with his phone and reading a magazine. He didn't notice her when she walked up, so she rapped her knuckles on the dark wood, dumping her bags at her feet. The man pulled one ear bud from his ear. "Help you?"

"Yeah, I'm Michael Shafer. I'm here to do a big piece for lobby. Do you know where they want me to work?"

"Oh yeah, Shafer…" he said, picking up a clipboard and scrolling the names. "Right this way. They've got you over here."

Michael hefted her tool bag and her duffel and followed the man as he walked briskly past a wall that was in the process of being removed. As she rounded the corner, a grin spread across her face. Under a nondescript gray tarp must be sitting a huge hunk of marble, hers for the taking. Her fingers tingled as she neared the middle of the space and grabbed a corner of the tarp from the floor.

"The name's Jim if you need anything. They want guests to sign in and out, so if you're expecting someone, just let me know."

Michael ignored Jim as she pulled hard on the heavy fabric and her medium was revealed. Becoming acquainted with a new medium was a special moment for Michael. She rubbed her hands over the raw edges of the marble, mentally taking measurements and deciding which angles would work best. Jim huffed and walked out of the space.

Michael sighed and pulled off her polo shirt, leaving her in a white tank and old jeans. She also removed her shoes. She hated working with shoes on. Turning around and surveying the room for the first time, Michael realized Marguerite had honored her every request. Two entire walls of the room were windows, letting in large amounts of natural light. There was a large wooden workbench with a corkboard hung above it on the wall nearest the door. Deciding to get right to work, Michael pulled out her tools and arranged them by size on the workbench. Next she pulled out the dozens of sketches she had been working on. Glancing at the marble, she opened a pack of push pins from the table. She could already feel her ideas coming to life.

Tacking papers to the corkboard, Michael stood back to examine the numerous angles she had previously sketched her subject from. The woman she envisioned was begging for life, and Michael couldn't wait to oblige. Scrutinizing her sketches for a moment longer, Michael grabbed her tools and went to work.

❖

"What the hell do you mean she left? No good-bye? No nothing? What the fuck? I'll kill her!" Morgan screeched, banging her fist on the top of their favorite table at Nine's. "After all that? She just left you?" she continued, anger contorting her delicate facial features. Jess was too heartbroken to scold Morgan for her language.

"I don't know why she left. It was the most amazing night of my entire life, and I wake up in the morning to find a drawing and a note that says 'I'm sorry.' That's it!" Jess bit her lip. It had been nearly a week since Michael left, and after no word from her, Jess's anger had turned to despair. And she felt ashamed and embarrassed to boot. Michael hadn't even contacted her. *Good gracious!* She was not going to contact Michael. Her heart was in a zillion pieces, and she looked like a before picture from a makeover, but she still had a shred of pride.

Morgan had come over to Jess's apartment that afternoon, demanding that Jess tell her what was going on. "You look like a zombie. All you do is listen to Radiohead and read *Wuthering Heights*. Are you going to start adopting cats? What the hell is going on?" she had said, flopping on the couch, determined to get some answers.

"I don't even like cats. And there is nothing wrong with a little nineties alternative entertainment." Pretending to tidy her already immaculate living room and putting Emily Bronte back on the book shelf, Jess hoped Morgan wouldn't notice all the framed pictures of Michael and her were facedown. Jess was normally pretty neat, but to keep her mind off Michael, she had taken up cleaning in her free time. Deep cleaning. Like cleaning the grooves in the wood of her coffee table with a toothbrush kind of cleaning.

"You can't miss Michael that much," Morgan snorted. At

this comment Jess sank into the sofa, folding her legs under her, and stared at Morgan. The ever-present headache returned and exhaustion made her hands shake. Most nights she would lie awake thinking about Michael's smile, Michael's hands, her lips. On the nights she wasn't on the brink of orgasm just from reliving her night with Michael, she would cry and eat piles of sweets. She was grumpy and irritable. She couldn't concentrate and she was lashing out, but she wouldn't lie to her friend and she was tired of avoiding her. Anger began to bubble up, roiling into rage in a matter of seconds.

"You want to know what's wrong? I slept with Michael! We slept together and it was incredible. It was life changing. And then she left. I am completely and utterly in love with her! We had sex, and we spent all night pleasuring each other, then she got up and left me alone in her bed the next morning to start her new life in New York. That's what's wrong!" After the outburst, Jess clamped her mouth.

Morgan stood there, staring at Jess in disbelief. "Come with me," Morgan said, pulling Jess by the hand. "We're going to Nine's, and you're going to tell me everything."

So here they sat, three hours later, way past Jess's bedtime. She had relived every amazing moment of her lovemaking with Michael. Well, almost every moment. She left out the most intimate details, like the fact that she had five orgasms and the fact that her throat was sore the next day from screaming Michael's name. She also left out the fact that she'd had no idea how flexible she was until that night, but from her abbreviated version of the story, Morgan got the idea.

"Morgan, it was...I don't know. Just think of the most epic thing you can imagine—"

"Oh, that Meatloaf music video. Totally. You know, the one where he's the beast and that chick is beauty and there's an orchestra." Morgan pumped her fist in the air. "So epic."

"Yeah, yeah I get it. It was like that. But sex. And no Meatloaf."

"Well, call her dumb ass." Morgan leaned forward with a dumbfounded look, as if the answer to this problem were that simple.

"No!" Jess shot back with a glare.

Morgan held up her hands in apology. "I'm sorry. I don't mean to be insensitive, but you can't let her ruin this. You deserve happiness. And if Michael isn't the one to give it to you, you damn well deserve an explanation."

"I just can't," Jess whispered weakly. "I can't talk to her, knowing how much that night meant to me, and knowing she doesn't feel the same way. I just can't do it, Morgan. Can you understand? She's the love of my life, and she doesn't want to be with me. She regrets our night together. I don't want to hear that from her." She finished the last words in a scratchy sob. She was glad they were among the last of the patrons at Nine's, otherwise she would feel that much more like a blubbering idiot.

"Oh, sweetie." Morgan left her side of the booth and scooted in close to Jess.

Jess pulled Morgan toward her into a tight hug.

❖

A month had gone by since Michael had spoken to Jess. A month since they had made love. Michael spent her days sculpting and working to exhaustion so she could fall into a deep, dreamless sleep. On most days, especially sixteen- or eighteen-hour days where she had barely taken time to eat, sleep would come easily. But it was on nights like tonight, when her mind was racing and her body was wired, that she had the most trouble finding rest.

The New York skyline at night was so terrific that Michael had taken to sleeping with the drapes open. Tonight she stood looking out the floor-to-ceiling windows, wearing only her black briefs. Below, the tiny cars moving in straight lines reminded her that there were so many people in the world, but she had never felt so alone. She had even begun avoiding speaking to her mother because she too often asked about Jess.

Camille called her often, but she hadn't told her about what happened with Jess. She knew exactly what Camille's reaction would be. She thought Michael and Jess belonged together. In some tiny space in the back of her heart, Michael had hoped that was true. But after a month with no word from Jess, Michael could only assume Jess had written her off. Was she angry that Michael had allowed their night together to happen? Had she come to terms with the fact that their friendship would be forever changed and they should probably just go their separate ways?

How did Jess feel about all this? Maybe she could open the lines of communication…just a little. Hopping on the bed, Michael grabbed her cell phone, opened a blank message, and typed "I miss you." It took her several minutes to get up enough courage to press send, and at the last second, she pressed cancel instead.

With more force than she intended, Michael threw her phone against the wall and watched it break in half. Cursing at her cowardice, Michael went over to the dresser and poured a shot. She had started keeping tequila in the hotel room to help her sleep. Perhaps a sleep aid would have worked better, but it wouldn't help to numb her feelings. Michael sat on the edge of the bed and downed the shot. Then she cradled her head in her hands.

CHAPTER SIXTEEN

Y ou're not wearing that, are you?" Morgan spat as she entered the living room of Jess's apartment. She looked Jess up and down as she put her purse on the counter.

"What's wrong with this?" Jess shrugged her shoulders and spun in a small circle. Okay, so she hadn't tried very hard, but these days Jess was more concerned with comfort than what looked good. As long as there were no stains or holes, it would work for her. Tonight was the first time she agreed to go out with the girls since Michael left. A night at home with Stephen King in one hand and a wineglass in the other was much more appealing.

"You look like you just crawled out of bed...for the first time in two weeks. At least your hair is brushed." Morgan made a disgusted face. "Are your teeth?" She held her hand out for Jess to precede her into the bedroom. "You might not want a woman, but I don't want you to scare them all away. Go change."

"Fine, but I'm only trying on one more thing." Jess went back into her closet. *Why do I have so many clothes?* She grabbed the dark blue dress she'd worn to Michael's last gallery showing and threw it on the floor. *Nope.* Pulling on the sleeve of her billowy pink blouse, she decided against that too.

She wore that the last time she and Michael went to the antique furniture market. Scooting to the very back of her closet, Jess saw a forest green dress she bought online a few years ago. She couldn't even remember the last time she wore it. *Perfect.*

"Have you heard from the Asshole Stud Muffin?" This was Morgan's latest nickname for Michael since Jess had discussed their night together and the way Michael disappeared afterward. Much to Jess's relief, the names were becoming less and less offensive.

In her heart, Jess knew Morgan was trying to be supportive, but the last thing she wanted to discuss was Michael. "I would have told you if I had. I have agreed to go out tonight, so can we please not talk about it?"

"I don't want to talk about her," Morgan said casually, and under her breath added, "I want to kill her."

"Morgan." Jess left the closet dressed and gave Morgan a scowl. As angry as she was at Michael, she still felt a need to protect her. *I love her.* It felt strange saying it to herself, but it made it all the more real and made Michael's absence in her life that much more acute.

"Fine. Sorry. No more mentions of the Deadbeat Douche Bag." Morgan hopped off the bed and ran from the room to avoid the sweater Jess threw at her.

❖

Nine's was no more crowded than usual and Jess was relieved that the music for the drag show had already started. She wouldn't have to talk to anyone too much. It helped a lot to know that her friends were there for her, but Jess wanted to be at home, not watching the smiling faces of lesbians in love or girls flirting with potential bed partners. At Morgan's suggestion that Jess sleep with someone else to get her mind off Michael, Jess felt nauseous. She didn't want to erase the memory of Michael's hands with the unfamiliar touch of some stranger. After getting her drink from Robin, she made her way through the crowd toward the stage as Morgan stopped to speak to a few friends.

"Hey, we're over here, Jess!" Stevie said over the music as Jess changed directions toward their regular booth. "So glad you could come!" Stevie seemed in good spirits, probably due to the barely legal girl draped on her arm. Jess tried not to scowl.

"Me too. I've been really busy." *Reevaluating everything I thought I could trust in my life.* Jess set her drink down and scooted into the booth. She was relieved that Camille was talking to a couple to their right. Maybe she wouldn't notice Jess had arrived. Jess liked Camille, but other than their closest friends, they ran in completely different circles. The only thing they really had in common was Michael, and Jess felt sure that would be at the top of the list of things to make small talk about.

The stage was set in the middle of the back wall and was visible from most of the booths on the upper end of the bar past the dance floor. Jess almost wished they were closer to the performers. Back here they would be able to talk over the music. Talk and ask questions. She felt afraid anyone might ask her why she hadn't been out lately or if she had heard from Michael. But she had to do this. She could do this. It was for Morgan. To help Morgan feel like Jess wanted to rejoin the land of the living.

People scooted their chairs back to their tables to wait for the show to begin, and before Jess could think of a good reason to leave the table, Camille leaned over, trying to be heard over the music. "It's been a while. How are you? Missing Michael?" Camille asked.

Jess set her drink down, sure she was going to drop it at the mention of Michael's name. Jess's eyes darted between Camille and the drag queen on stage, dressed like a peacock and performing to "Total Eclipse of the Heart." Michael had taken her to see Bonnie Tyler two years ago for her birthday. Another memory. Jess's throat tightened and she stood, nearly knocking the table over.

"I...I, um...I have to go to the bathroom." Jess raced through the throng of people and to the empty bathroom. Turning the faucet on full blast, she splashed cold water on her face. She hadn't been wearing makeup lately—no fear of messing that up.

Michael was everywhere. Jess couldn't escape her. Not in her closet, not at Nine's, not even in her dreams. Her friendship with Michael encompassed and defined her life. Her heart belonged to Michael, but now her body did too. Nothing was hers anymore. Just as she finished drying her face with a rough brown paper towel, Camille came into the bathroom with a concerned look.

"Are you okay?" She put her hand on Jess's shoulder and looked at her in the mirror.

"Have you talked to Michael?" Jess asked before she could stop herself, trying to keep the anger and pain from her voice. She had to know. Had to know if she was okay. She had to know if she was happy. Was she enjoying her work? Was she making friends? Was she going out with friends? Was she fucking someone?

"I...well, yes. I've spoken to her a few times. She's been working nonstop and she's ahead of schedule. I was actually going to ask if you could talk to her. She needs to slow down. I don't want her worn out for the opening," Camille said with a small smile. She obviously thought this was a change in subject from whatever Jess was so upset about. Well, that couldn't be further from the truth.

"She didn't tell you, did she?" Jess let out a slow breath and counted to ten, just as she told her students to do when they became angry or upset. Why should it be such a secret? Was Michael that ashamed of their night together that she didn't even tell one of her best friends?

"Didn't tell me what?"

"Forget it. She can tell you herself." Jess stormed past Camille, not meeting her eyes.

Camille put a hand on Jess's arm as she tried to pass. "Jess, what is it? If there's something up with Michael, then I need to know. Especially if it's going to affect her career."

Jess looked down at Camille's hand and decided just because Michael was ashamed of what happened between them didn't mean she should be. And she wasn't.

"We slept together," Jess said without any indication of anger. She heard Camille gasp. "We spent the night together and then she walked away. I haven't heard from her since. I can assure you, it won't affect her career." Jess left the bathroom and headed home.

❖

"She must be pissed about something," Michael mumbled to herself as she put her cell phone down. Camille had been calling her nonstop for almost a week, and Michael was steadfastly avoiding her. Camille wasn't leaving messages, so it couldn't be too important. Michael stuffed the rest of her sandwich in her mouth, wiped her hands on a napkin, and readied her tools for detail work. Michael didn't want to be nagged right now. The last few weeks she had not been able to sleep, and aside from grabbing stuff from the fabulous sandwich shop across the street, she hadn't been buying food. It was hard to sleep at night and even harder to wake up and pull herself from the warmth of the bed and the warmth of Jess's memory. The best part of the day was the first second she was awake, before she could fully comprehend her surroundings. In those precious moments, she could still feel Jess's naked body wrapped around hers.

After losing her nerve once when attempting to contact Jess through text, Michael threw herself even harder into sculpting, but it wasn't working anymore. She daydreamed when she should be sculpting, and fantasized when she should be sketching. Everything made her think of Jess. While she was ahead of schedule the previous week, she'd be lucky to finish by the opening. Bursts of energy struck her but soon her hands would tire, and the next thing she knew she would be obsessing about Jess again. It was crazy. She was crazy.

Wiping sweat from her brow, Michael knelt next to the bottom of the sculpture in a catcher's stance. Her quads bunched and pulled the fabric of her shorts tight against her thighs, but this was the best angle to remove large chunks of stone from the base of her sculpture. Michael put her weight on the balls of her feet and, using her upper body as leverage against her pick and hammer, she pounded away at the last remaining rough edge of marble. This was the final section of labor-intensive sculpting before she would be moving on to the detail work. While she was relieved to see the sculpture take form, she would miss the exhausting, mind-numbing work that allowed her to forget everything except the burning of her muscles, the aching of her hands.

With just a little over a month until the opening, the most intricate and difficult sculpting work was still ahead. It was easy to make abstract pieces with no real detail, but she wanted this piece to come alive in the detail. When people entered the lobby of *Le Femme* magazine, Michael wanted them to experience the beauty and presence of Jess. Michael stood, brushing dust from her shorts, and slipped her tools into her tool belt. Their relationship was done, but at least this sculpture could preserve Jess forever, in a way others could also appreciate. It seemed only fitting that the most important sculpture of her career thus far would mirror the most important person in her life. She knew nothing would ever compare to the real thing, but she wanted people to be as captivated by this work of art as Michael herself was by the woman herself. Michael knew this was a dangerous line of thinking, especially since she needed to at least finish the details of the feet before she headed back to her hotel for the night.

Pulling the bag of detailing tools from the table, Michael glanced at the sculpture's undefined feet to assess where to begin. Closing her eyes to visualize the final product, she was struck in the stomach by the visceral memory of Jess's heels digging into her back as she thrust her hips hard into Jess, driving them both over the edge. Sweat had dripped from her brow onto Jess's breasts and Jess had screamed her name. Yes, it was their first time as lovers, but Michael felt as if she had been born to touch Jess's body. She felt as though she was put on this earth to do nothing more than caress Jess and love every inch of her form. As the memory rolled through her, it caused a burning in her lower belly, and Michael braced her arms on the work table and tried to get her body under control. She felt guilty becoming aroused when she thought about Jess because her emotions were about so much more than sex. But the sex had been…astounding. Michael had never come so easily, or so frequently. It had become increasingly obvious throughout their night together that Michael's deep and almost obsessive love for Jess when combined with her ever-present attraction made for the most powerful and intense sexual experience possible. Everything felt new, wonderful, and powerful, as if she had been reborn into another body. A body that was called to answer every sexual desire of Jess's body.

After a few deep breaths, Michael picked up her carver's drill and knelt by the sculpture's feet to begin working. As she inspected the head of the drill she heard someone enter the lobby door. Michael turned to find Marguerite walking toward her.

"Hello, Michael," she said in her sultry tone. Marguerite was incredibly attractive, and Michael didn't think she tried to be seductive or sexy, but she was just the same. Under normal circumstances Michael would be intrigued by a woman like Marguerite, but Michael was beginning to realize she was never going to feel "normal" again.

"Hi, Marguerite," Michael said, jumping up and wiping the dust from her hands and clothes. She wanted to make sure she could answer any of Marguerite's questions, so she went over to the table and picked up some of her sketches and notes.

"I'm starting to detail now. Does everything look okay? I'm on schedule and things are looking good," Michael said nervously, before Marguerite had a chance to ask.

Marguerite began to appraise the sculpture from top to bottom as she walked gracefully and with confidence completely around it. Michael was ready for any critiques Marguerite had to offer and would adjust her work accordingly. She knew Marguerite to be incredibly shrewd and blunt. Working in the lobby of the office afforded her the opportunity to see Marguerite interact with others. When addressing the construction workers and contractors, she was always respectful and polite, but she made her wants known. Rubbing the back of her neck, Michael watched Marguerite's face for signs of approval and awaited her reply.

"The pose is strong. I look forward to an expression that matches. I feel confident you will deliver on your promise of fierceness." Marguerite glanced at the sketches Michael held, and then the dozens of others tacked to the corkboard and spread across the work table. "She is your lover, no?" asked Marguerite, arching an eyebrow.

"What? Who? No." Shocked, Michael stumbled with her words. While readying herself for any input Marguerite had about her work, she was not prepared for such a personal question. She was about to ask who Marguerite was referring to, but she didn't need to. It was obvious that this beauty was sculpted from Michael's heart. The sketches were pointless, as she never looked at them when working. She didn't need to.

Rather than probe further, Marguerite just crossed her arms and stared at Michael. It had not taken long for Michael to see how Marguerite had become such a successful businesswoman. An authoritative glare from those crystal blue eyes would make even a hardened criminal fess up.

Michael resisted the urge to shuffle her feet and look down. She held Marguerite's gaze and spoke of Jess for the first time to anyone since their night together. "No. Not lover. Her name is Jess. My best friend. And the love of my life. We were together once before I came here. But we haven't spoken since," Michael blurted, turning away from Marguerite. She pulled her T-shirt on over her sweat-soaked and dusty tank top. With all the thoughts running through her mind, she knew she wouldn't get much more work done tonight.

"*La douleur exquise…*" Marguerite said, almost to herself.

"Pardon?" Michael asked, not sure if the words were meant for her.

"A French phrase. Roughly translated, it means 'the exquisite pain.' The emotional ache of wanting someone you know you cannot have."

"Aptly put." Michael sighed in response as she felt the tissue around her heart ache.

"Why have you not spoken with her?" Marguerite's voice remained soft. It seemed strange to hear her use such a gentle voice. Michael had never heard it from her before.

"She doesn't love me. She never has. It was a mistake," Michael continued as she began to put her tools away and tidy up her work area.

"Do you know, Michael, that I considered seducing you when I first saw you enter the restaurant. You are so capable and strong. Yet you present yourself in a humble and kind way. It is very intoxicating," Marguerite said, as she wandered closer to Michael. "Do you know what stopped me, Michael? What kept me from taking what I wanted?"

"No." Michael asked, feeling even more shocked. Michael thought back to a time in her life not that long ago when she would have gladly spent a few hours in the arms of this attractive near stranger. And it occurred to her in this very moment that if she were to sleep with any other woman, all she would think about was Jess. And no one would compare.

Marguerite took her manicured index finger and placed it right on the sketch of her sculpture's face. "Her."

Michael's gaze fell to her sketches pinned all over the wall. They didn't even do her justice. She had never found a way to capture Jess's true beauty in any medium she had tried.

"This is the woman who holds your heart. It is a cruel woman who would sleep with you when she knows how dearly you love her. Especially if she does not return your feelings."

Michael was on the verge of getting angry. Her possessive and nearly chauvinistic side would surely rear its ugly head at any comment that would suggest Jess was at fault for any of this. There was not a cruel bone in Jess's body. "It wasn't like that. She doesn't know how I feel. I've never told her. I don't know why she slept with me." This was proving to be a very insightful conversation indeed. Until she spoke those words, Michael had never considered why Jess slept with *her*. It was true she wondered how often Jess slept with people she considered friends. *But why me? Why now?* Her own actions had been much easier to explain. Once Michael tasted Jess's lips, she had to possess her.

"She doesn't know the depth of your feelings? Well, then it is you who are cruel. How could you deny her a love this strong?" Marguerite put her hand out and held Michael's hands. "A love that creates such beauty, a love flowing from your hands." She slowly moved one hand up and laid it on Michael's chest. "And in your heart."

Michael lifted her eyebrows and stared at the ceiling in an effort to keep the tears welling in her eyes from falling. Was she denying Jess the love she would so happily give to her? A love she was letting eat her alive?

"But she doesn't..." Michael began.

"How do you know? What if she does?"

❖

Turning her pillow over for the third time in as many minutes, Jess kept trying to find a comfortable position to sleep in. It was after one a.m. and Jess knew she would feel awful the next day if she didn't at least get a few decent hours of sleep. She especially needed to be well-rested for the last day of school. She planned a class party at the end of each school year. Parents were invited, and there were snacks and balloons to celebrate her students' accomplishments. All things considered, her school year had managed to go well. The kids made surprising progress, and she was proud to be sending two students on to middle school.

She wondered what Michael was doing now. Probably sleeping. Jess selfishly hoped she was sleeping instead of out with friends...or a girlfriend. The thought sickened Jess. Michael was a flesh-and-blood woman, and after their night together, Jess knew she was an incredibly passionate one. How long would it be before Michael found someone else to pleasure? Michael kissing and touching her until the only thing that could escape from her lips would be Michael's name?

Jess flopped onto her back, swore, and threw a pillow across the room. Staring up at the painting above her bed, she was tempted to pull it off its nail and throw that across the room as well. The painting of fireflies floating underneath a willow tree had been a present from Michael when Jess moved into this apartment. Jess remembered feeling so moved, especially when she found out Michael had built the frame for the canvas herself. The summer evenings in Dogwood Bluff were full of fireflies, and they would catch bug after bug until they couldn't find any more. Jess felt cruel putting them in jars the way some kids did, and they developed a catch and release method when it came to the glowing insects. Jess's heart began to ache even more when she thought of Michael and the way she had let those fragile bugs fly out of her hands as a child, just because Jess wanted her to. No matter what Jess wanted from her, she would never hold Michael back from what she wanted to do in life. She had to let her go too.

CHAPTER SEVENTEEN

I'm looking for Michael Shafer."
Michael's head snapped up as she heard a woman say her name from the lobby in an aggravated tone. In a rush she put her tools down on the floor and jumped up to meet the woman in the lobby before she barged into the work area. The construction workers had draped some dark green plastic from the ceiling to give her privacy to work, and she rushed to move it aside and secure it closed behind her before anyone could enter.

"I don't care if I'm not on some goddamned list! I'm going in there!" The woman's loud voice echoed in the nearly empty space as she glared at Jim. She was standing in front of his tall desk with her arms crossed, tapping her expensive-looking shoe on the tile floor. It was around noon and Michael was relieved most of the crew was on their lunch break. The men had left in a rush, leaving tools, paint, and ladders placed haphazardly all over the open space.

Oh, no.

Sara had the same lustrous brown hair as Jess, but the similarities ended there. Unlike Jess's voluptuous curves, Sara was short with a slight frame. Her eyes were brown, not deep sapphire like her sister's. It had been years since Michael had seen Sara, and in all their time growing up together she had never heard her so angry.

"You," Sara snapped as she saw Michael approach, her eyes wide and furious. "We need to talk."

Before she responded, a dreadful thought entered Michael's brain. What if something had happened to Jess? An accident? "Sara, what is it? Is Jess okay?" Michael asked. All thoughts of awkwardness and what Jess must think of her fled from her mind. If something had happened to Jess, Michael would never forgive herself for walking out on her.

Sara again glared at Jim, who excused himself for a smoke break.

"Physically, yes. Jess is fine," she replied in a less hateful voice.

Now in front of Jim's desk a few feet away from Sara, Michael sank down against the heavy wood to sit on the floor and rubbed her face roughly with her hands as she let the relief wash over her. Then the rest of what Sara had said sank in. "What do you mean 'physically'?"

"What the hell have you done to my sister, you asshole?" Sara screamed as Michael jumped up and backed away from her, holding her hands up in exasperation.

"What...nothing...I mean..." Michael stammered. Dropping her hands to her sides, Michael was not going to fight off Sara's anger. She had every right to be angry. So did Jess.

"First you won't talk to her about the kiss, then you sleep with her, then you won't speak to her? Do I have everything straight?" Sara counted the events off on her fingertips, her voice had lowered considerably but was still icy.

"No, I...wait, kiss. What kiss? With Stevie? Why would I want to talk to her about that?" Michael asked, getting angry herself. She understood Sara coming over here to defend her sister, or even to scold Michael for making a mess of things, but no one was going to try to make her feel bad for self-preservation. Michael was not going to stand by and be forced to endure discussions about Jess and Stevie's sexual chemistry. Had she slept with Stevie that night? Michael's head began to hurt as she ran through all the possibilities and mistakes that were mounting up in front of her like trash at a landfill.

"You're a real asshole, Shafer. How drunk were you that night? The only person she willingly kissed that night was you." Sara set her briefcase down and walked around the desk to sit in Jim's cushy office chair, apparently intending to stay for a while.

"Kissed me...Jess kissed me?" Michael shut her eyes tight and rubbed her forehead. Bits and pieces of that night had returned to her, but a lot of it was still unclear. *Wait...*

"The dream..." Michael said to herself as she rubbed her bottom lip. The dream of kissing Jess had been so real, so vivid. The taste of Jess's lips, the feel of her skin. Even the smell of her. It was the most realistic dream Michael had ever had. What if it hadn't just been a dream?

"Dream? Yeah, like a dream come true for Jess. It changed everything. So then you sleep with her, and what, forget she exists?" Sara barked. She must have noticed the deeply wounded look in Michael's eyes at that comment because she again lowered her tone. "Jess is one of the most wonderful, positive, and selfless people I've ever known. Lately she will hardly take my calls, she's lost weight, she was even missing work until summer break started. I don't know what happened between you two, or what you even want to happen, Michael, but you need to talk to her. You need to tell her how you feel because this is killing her. And she deserves better."

"I know what she deserves!" Michael yelled, angry at Sara for doubting her intentions with Jess. Angry at herself for the way she had treated Jess. "She deserves so much more than I can offer her." Michael's voice sounded small and far away even to her own ears.

"Then you need to tell her that." Sara stood and put her hand on Michael's arm. Michael shied away from her touch, she was so ashamed of herself. "You look like shit. Get your act together and talk to her."

After Michael asked some obligatory questions about how Sara was doing, Michael walked her out, hailed her a cab, and said good-bye.

Returning to her work space, Michael stared at the floor trying to make sense of what Sara had told her. Blood rushed through her ears; her hands and even her legs shook. She sat and tried to control the nausea threatening to overtake her. If the dream had been real…then maybe Jess had wanted to make love to her that night. Maybe Jess hadn't regretted it in the morning.

And Michael had just left her.

"I just left her," Michael whispered out loud. "I left her with a note and a damned drawing." More anger at herself tore through her as she shoved her sketches to the floor and held her head in her hands.

Images of Jess filled her mind in a rush. Not just their night together, but Jess as a teenager cheering for Michael as she played point guard on the varsity basketball team. The time when Jess helped wash her first car because it was so filthy. She would never forget the sight of Jess in that little pink bikini top and cut-offs. Michael recalled the time when she had the flu in college, and Jess had come up from FSU to stay with her, unmindful of her own health as she had cared for Michael. She even went to the crappy dorm kitchen to make her mother's homemade chicken noodle soup. She pictured Jess with her students. The way she treated them, as if they were all perfect. She pictured Jess's eyes lighting up when she entered a room or touched people lightly as she spoke.

Jess was not the kind of girl you slept with and tossed away. Michael would never forgive herself for treating her in such a way. How could she do anything to make Jess feel unwanted when she was anything but? Distancing herself from Jess, denying her feelings, convincing herself Jess thought their night together was a mistake...these were all things Michael had done to spare her own feelings. She had not once taken Jess's feelings into consideration. Everything she had done to deny her feelings and protect their friendship, it was all for herself. How could she be so selfish?

Marguerite's words echoed in her mind. Was she denying Jess her love? Would Jess even want her after everything? It didn't matter anymore. Michael was tired of fighting it. Of fighting Jess. She needed to come clean and tell Jess everything. She deserved better than Michael could ever offer her...but she also deserved the truth.

❖

That night Michael called Marguerite's secretary and asked for a morning appointment with her. The secretary, a woman with a strong but professional New York accent, had said the only available time Marguerite had would be right at the beginning of the workday. Although Michael still had much to do, she had agreed right away to the meeting.

Now, standing in the elevator of the new *La Femme* headquarters, staring at the numbers on the digital display go up, Michael began to feel a little nervous about the meeting. She knew it was a long shot and that Marguerite might not agree and simply tell her she was insane, but she had to give it a shot. It was for Jess. It was for her forgiveness.

As the elevator doors slid open, Michael clutched her portfolio tightly in her hands. In it she had laid out her plans and was about to throw her heart and future into Marguerite's hands. She said good morning to the secretary, who waved her toward a gigantic pair of oak doors with modern stainless steel handles.

Michael knocked three times and heard Marguerite's muffled voice tell her to enter.

"Michael. You look as though your mood has improved since the last time we spoke," Marguerite said, standing behind the most massive desk Michael had ever seen. For a moment she wondered if it had been built in the office. It was so big she knew it wouldn't have fit through the door in one piece; Michael often took notice of room dimensions that others didn't notice. The office was impeccably decorated. Large pieces of modern art, some of which Michael recognized, hung from three walls. The wall behind Marguerite's desk showcased an amazing view of the New York City skyline. To the right was a large conference table littered with magazines, sketches, and advertisements. Michael assumed this was where the powers that be would meet to decide the contents in the next issue of *La Femme*.

As Marguerite rounded the large desk, she motioned for Michael to follow her to the left side of the office, which had an impressive bar, lined with many top-shelf brands of liquor and rum. Michael was surprised someone would keep so much alcohol in her office. She guessed everyone was entitled to a little downtime…even if it was in her own office.

"What brings you to see me, Michael? I stopped by your space on my way up, and I must say, she is looking fantastic. I assume we are still on schedule?" Marguerite brought out two champagne flutes and held one toward Michael. "Mimosa?"

"No. Thank you. A little too early." She gave Marguerite a

tight smile. Not to mention the fact that Michael had promised herself to cut back since she found out about her kiss with Jess. She didn't think her drinking was out of control, but the fact that something of that magnitude could happen without her being fully aware of it scared her a little.

"Thank you for seeing me on such short notice. And I apologize for getting so…emotional last time we spoke."

"Oh, no need. Emotions run deep within us all. Why should any of us be ashamed?" Marguerite continued to make herself a mimosa and poured Michael some plain orange juice in one of the flutes. She rounded the bar and sat down on a low plush couch, indicating with a nod of her head that Michael should join her. "I know you did not come to see me to discuss emotions." She sipped her drink. "What is on your mind, Michael?"

Michael took a long swig of her juice before she began. Now that the moment was upon her to ask for Marguerite's help, she wished perhaps there was some champagne in her drink after all.

"In a way I guess I am here to talk about emotion. One in particular. I'm in love with Jessica. She is my life. My muse. As you can see from my work." Michael looked away. Openness was not something she was used to when it came to discussing her feelings, especially her feelings for Jess.

Her resolve to ask for Marguerite's help was about to crumble, but she knew she had to go on. If she wanted any chance at Jess's forgiveness or a future with her, it would depend on how well she was able to convey her feelings now. She had to make this count.

"I need her to forgive me," Michael felt flustered. "I need her to understand that I…I—"

"Worship the ground she walks on?" Marguerite supplied, as if it were obvious.

Michael looked up, praying for the courage to continue and put words to her feelings. "Yes. The ground she walks on. The air she breathes. She is everything to me and I need her back in my life."

Marguerite smiled. "What is it you need from me?"

❖

Two hours later after pleading her case and showing Marguerite her new sketches, Michael sat quietly, waiting for a response.

"It is quite unconventional for the gathering we had in mind," Marguerite began.

Michael's shoulders slumped. "I understand."

"But…" Marguerite continued, a trace of a smile playing with the corners of her mouth. "I love it."

Michael smiled as big as she dared while trying to remain professional. "Marguerite, I can't…I mean…Thank you."

"I have one condition, Michael." Marguerite held up one finger and returned Michael's smile.

"Anything…"

"You must allow me to share your story with our *La Femme* readers."

"You've got a deal." Michael stuck out her hand and grabbed Marguerite's with what she hoped was not too much force.

"See the head contractor, Marlowe. Tell him to do as you say. I trust you, Michael. You have made this project real. Sharing this at our opening will make it as real for everyone else as it is for you."

❖

It had been almost six weeks since her night with Michael, but only minutes since Jess last thought of her. The beginning of the summer had been rough and Jess was sad to say good-bye to another school year, if only because work kept her mind off Michael. She found it easy to occupy her time with preparing lessons and activities for the upcoming school year. The principal allowed her to get into her classroom early even though the custodians were not completely through with their summer cleaning. The days were getting easier. The nights were a different story. She had become a regular at her local branch of the Atlanta Public Library and read nearly the entire best-sellers list. Next she concentrated on mysteries, making sure to avoid any titles that alluded to romance. She would read until her eyes grew weary, trying to escape into another world, a world where she wasn't overcome with loneliness. Reading occupied her mind until she could no longer focus on the words, until she would turn out the light and pray for sleep. On the nights where sleep came easily, Jess was plagued by dreams of her one night with Michael. Tangled sheets, sweat-slicked bodies, carnal moans. On more than one occasion she found herself startled awake. The only way to assuage the hunger was to take matters into her own hands, but her orgasms were hard won, and not nearly worth the effort.

One particular night, Jess was awoken by a dream of swimming with Michael in the lake at Dogwood Bluff. The starring role of the fantasy was Michael's strong, adept hands. She could feel them everywhere—on her face, her breasts, her legs, tangled in her hair. She had never thought of her scalp as an erogenous zone until Michael's fingers had rubbed and gently scraped nearly every inch of her head. Glancing at the clock, she saw it was nearly five a.m. and decided to go ahead and get up. No more sleep after that dream.

After a quick shower, Jess poured herself a cup of almond milk and forced herself to eat some of a blueberry muffin. As she headed to the table, she picked up the growing stack of mail from the counter. Plopping down at the kitchen table with a groan, she sorted through the mass of papers and magazines. Junk. Bill. Junk. Card. Junk. As she continued to sort, one envelope in particular caught her eye. It was a heavy card stock envelope in an iridescent lavender color. Baby shower maybe? There was no return address.

Putting aside the other mail, Jess gently pulled open the flap and pulled out the card.

To Miss Jessica Gable
The Board of Directors of Le Femme
cordially invite you to a festive evening
celebrating the unveiling of our original lobby sculpture.
Please RSVP by the 28th of July.
La Femme Magazine, LLC.

Jess nearly fell out of her chair. Was Michael reaching out to her? Her mind raced as she considered all the possibilities. Surely not. Michael had not attempted to contact her in any way since they had been together. The list of invitees was probably made as soon as Michael was asked to complete this project. How could she possibly face Michael knowing that their night together meant nothing to her? Would Michael even want her to come?

Powering up her laptop, Jess made a decision. It didn't matter to her if Michael wanted her there or not, she would go. This was the perfect opportunity for Jess to say good-bye to Michael, get closure, and move on.

Tickets to New York were expensive, and she would need to buy something formal to wear. Something amazing. She could handle saying good-bye to Michael, she'd been doing okay so far, but she was going to make it truly difficult for Michael to watch her walk away. If Michael didn't want her, fine. But she was not about to shrivel up and disappear. This experience had taught her she had the strength to survive, and as much as her heart hurt, she took comfort in knowing she was strong enough to get through this, even without the support of her best friend. And one-time lover.

CHAPTER EIGHTEEN

Y ou look amazing," Sara said, as Jess entered the guest room in her second-floor walkup. When Jess told Sara she was coming for a visit, Sara was thrilled but also expressed her concern about Jess seeing Michael again. Jess assured Sara it was something she *had* to do, but now that the time had come, Jess wasn't as confident as before. Making up her mind in Atlanta had been easy, but the thought of actually being in the same room with Michael made her stomach flutter. She knew there couldn't be anything between them, but she didn't know how she could face those beautiful brown eyes and not melt on the spot.

The most amazing friendship in her life had culminated in an eye-opening and soul-gripping sexual encounter, and it was now all over. *Surreal.* It was hard to imagine her life without Michael, but she would have to. After all, they hadn't spoken in two months. Though Jess was heartbroken to know that the one person she felt a true connection with did not return her feelings, she knew she had to move on. There were things in her life that she wanted: a career, a loving partner, children. If Michael wasn't going to be a part of that, then so be it. Jess knew, however, she would never love any woman the way she loved Michael. Maybe she would adopt and be a single mom, but she was not about to deny herself the happy life she envisioned. She could move on. She would move on.

"I'm glad you look so good. She needs to know what she'll be missing," Sara grumbled, balancing a laundry basket on her hip and glancing at Jess from the doorway.

"Sara. That's not what this is about," Jess replied, with a lightness in her voice she didn't feel. Jess smoothed down the sides of her hair with a brush. She had pinned her hair up in a vintage victory roll and let the back fall into soft waves. Her short, bouncy bob had grown out and she enjoyed the new length as she looked at herself in the mirror. "I just need to do this. I need to face her so I can move on." Jess turned around, dabbing her eyes so her tears wouldn't mess with her makeup. "How do I look?" She wore an A-line dress with plum-colored lace detail at the neck.

Sara looked her younger sister up and down. "Beautiful. You look like Mom."

Jess enjoyed the compliment. Her mother had been the bravest and most beautiful woman. If Jess had an ounce of her fortitude, she knew she could get through the evening, and looking the part was a step in the right direction.

"Well, here goes nothing," Jess said, kissing Sara on the cheek. She grabbed her small clutch purse and headed for the door. "Will I have to walk far for a cab?"

"Just to the corner. There should be plenty this time of night. Are you sure you don't want me to go with you?"

"No. I need to do this by myself. And I need Michael to know I can do it by myself."

❖

The taxi slowly pulled up to the *La Femme* building as the procession of cars ahead emptied their guests out onto the sidewalk covered with a red carpet. Delicate white lights twinkled on all the trees and bushes. The humid New York air did nothing to detract from the beauty and freshness of the white hydrangeas flanking the entryway. Jess saw several celebrities she knew that had graced the cover of *La Femme* and many other beautiful people she assumed were models. It was obvious to Jess that this was a building that housed many businesses, but *La Femme* was indeed the most successful.

A large man with a neatly manicured beard opened the door for Jess and bid her good evening. He offered her a hand to help her out of the cab, and for a moment, Jess was embarrassed and feared she might be the only guest that showed up in a cab rather than a limo or private vehicle. Putting her insecurities aside and holding her head high, she headed into the lobby.

As she entered, she noticed a large kiosk to the right and a luxurious waiting area to the left with low gray couches and velvety purple pillows. Everything was decorated with pink and red flowers, not to mock femininity, she guessed, but to embrace the fact that this was a successful magazine run entirely by women. In the rear of the large lobby a grand staircase led to a bank of elevators. To the right of the staircase Jess could see the large sculpture covered by an equally large tarp.

A server walked by and offered her a glass of champagne. She mumbled a thank you as he walked away, amazed she was able to find her voice. Hoping the bubbly drink would help calm her nerves, she drank more than she probably should have in one swig. After glancing around to see if anyone had noticed, Jess almost dropped her glass when she spotted Michael across the room.

Michael was dressed immaculately in a tuxedo, but Jess was taken aback by how different she looked. She had lost weight. She looked tired. And…"heartbroken" was the word that came to mind. Excusing herself from to the circle of admirers gathered around her, Michael walked toward Jess with purpose.

Her breath caught. *I can't do this.*

Before Jess could formulate a thought or decide what she might say to Michael, a sultry voice sounded over the microphone. Michael looked toward the voice, then longingly at Jess, and turned on her heel to head toward the staircase, which served as a makeshift stage for the evening.

"Good evening," a beautiful woman said from behind the microphone. For the second time, Jess felt speechless. This woman was breathtaking.

Michael joined the woman on the staircase, standing just behind her and to the left. Jess swallowed. Was this the type of woman Michael had been spending time with while in New York? How could Jess compete with this woman? With this life? The woman continued to speak. "I am Marguerite LeBeau, editor and chief of *La Femme* magazine. Welcome to you all. And thank you for joining us on this auspicious occasion. *La Femme* began as a free publication for women nearly twelve years ago. And here we are today, opening a new headquarters as it has become one of the top three magazines for woman in this country."

While fighting her growing nausea and apprehension, Jess did register what hard work and determination it must have taken to build a magazine to such success. The people in the room stopped milling about, and all their attention was centered on the stage. If she attempted to leave now, she would surely interrupt the dedication of Michael's sculpture. She would wait until the breathtaking Aphrodite was done talking, then she'd make a run for it.

"One of the things that has made this possible is our

joined strength. Something women have an abundance of. With that thought, we now reveal our new and original lobby sculpture. A creation from the heart and mind of our sculptor, Ms. Michael Shafer."

As the crowd began applauding, Jess carefully backed toward the door. Before she got farther than the waiting area, two men pulled the tarp from the large sculpture, revealing Michael's creation.

Jess stopped cold as shock paralyzed her. Towering over the audience was the most realistic, gorgeous, and perfect piece of art she had ever seen. The elegant woman held a wide stance, most of the weight on her right leg in the front. Her left leg, just as strong, was planted a few feet back, her calf muscles bunching. Her shoulders were squared and her hands were curled into loose fists. She appeared strong, ready for battle, but a little tentative. Her eyes stared into the distance with a determined expression that didn't distract from the beauty of her face.

Speechless, Jess glanced through the throng of people, whose eyes were all riveted on the sculpture, and she spotted Michael. The sea of eyes focused on the beautiful creation, yet Michael's eyes were locked on Jess. It appeared to Jess that she was searching her face for approval. Did Michael doubt the faultless work she had created? And why on earth would she search out Jess for reassurance? Jess's heart ached and she returned her gaze at the sculpture.

Jess sucked in a breath as realization dawned. *It's me. That beautiful, strong, elegant woman is me.* The soft curves of her hips, her upturned nose, and the full lips. How had she not seen it sooner? It looked like a mirror image of herself. She looked strong and capable. She looked amazing. *Is this how Michael sees me?*

Jess couldn't think. She could hardly draw breath. Jess

walked closer to the sculpture to take in the intricate details of the carved marble, from the musculature to the tiny toenails. All of it showed incredibly hard work and an unbelievable passion.

As the applause died down, Marguerite continued, "Michael, will you please say a few words for us."

"This work…" Michael stopped, overcome with emotion.

Jess turned her eyes from the beautiful work of art to Michael. The love of her life.

"This sculpture depicts a woman with strength, beauty, elegance, and compassion. She represents what all women should strive to become. I am honored to bring her to life for *La Femme*. Thank you."

And with that, Michael left the stage and headed to another room beyond the statue. Where was she going? What did all this mean? The audience dispersed and continued to drink champagne and converse, most lingering near the enormous artwork. Jess began to follow Michael and saw she had darted into a room separated by a large, heavy curtain.

"We are all overcome and impressed by Ms. Shafer's sculpture, but she has offered to share some of her other works with us. The private gallery will open momentarily. This new collection of work is entitled *Everlasting*. Please have more champagne and enjoy the refreshments. Gaze at the detail and the powerful presence of our new sculpture. Enjoy!"

A private gallery showing? Jess was overwhelmed and so excited for Michael. She must have been even busier than anyone thought to complete other pieces for a gallery showing.

"Ms. Gable?" The same man from earlier with the well-manicured beard approached. "Your presence has been requested in the private gallery. Will you please accompany me?" he asked politely.

Jess didn't say anything but followed the man toward the

heavy curtain separating the lobby from the private gallery. Jess was too beaten down from the last two months to name the feelings bubbling up inside her. What did all this mean?

"Right through here, Ms. Gable," he said, as he held the heavy curtain aside for her.

It took several moments for Jess's eyes to adjust to the dim lighting, but she saw that at least thirty sketches and paintings adorned the walls in the small room, each with a small bulb illuminating it in a circle of light. She started with the wall to her immediate left, noting these were four sketches that appeared to have been pulled from a sketchbook, the rough, torn edges still visible. Upon closer inspection, she could tell they were all sketches of her in differing candid poses. If Jess had to guess, she'd say she had been no older than seventeen. *What is this exhibit?*

The next wall was a series of oil paintings. These were paintings of Jess with her students. While it was obvious Jess was with children in the paintings, Michael had done an incredible job making her face—with an expression of love— the central theme of the pieces. She recognized the images as framed pictures Michael had in her loft.

After taking in every detail she could, Jess looked around the room to see there were dozens and dozens of other pieces. All depicting her. Some on large canvases, some on cocktail napkins, ranging from their young high school years to as recent as a few months ago.

"I saved every drawing or sketch I ever did of you. I saved them all," Michael said quietly from behind her. She seemed to have appeared out of nowhere.

"These...but how did you..." Jess began, tears rimming her eyes. She didn't know if she could turn around to face Michael yet, but she could feel her everywhere.

Still standing behind her, Michael gently touched her

hand. "Shh. There's one more thing you need to see." Gripping Jess's hand, Michael led her to the back corner of the small gallery. With Michael now leading the way, Jess had no choice but to stare at her. What if this was just one of those wonderful dreams? A dream where she and Michael lived happily ever after, and then she woke up in a cold sweat? Jess squeezed Michael's warm fingers to make sure she was really there. As Jess moved her attention to the wall, Michael backed away as if not wanting to interrupt her perusal of the images.

There were three very large canvases that had been covered in bright reds and oranges, with stark black lines indicating the subjects of the art. These were the only works where the central theme was not Jess alone. Walking closer to the paintings, Jess ran her hands lovingly over the lines.

These were paintings of arms and legs, tangled in sheets. Lips during passionate kisses. And bodies intertwined. This was a depiction of Jess and Michael's night together. How perfectly she was able to convey the emotion, the explosion, the catharsis. Jess turned to face Michael.

"I don't..." Michael began, shoving her hands into the pockets of her tuxedo pants. "I mean, I can't begin to tell you how much I regret leaving you that morning. I can't begin to ask for your forgiveness. So I'm not going to. I'm just going to tell you...you mean the world to me. You are the world to me. You have been my best friend forever. But more than that, Jess, I don't know how you feel about me or what that night meant to you. But I love you. I love you with everything I am. I always have. I can't deny it anymore. And even if you don't want my love, it's yours just the same."

It seemed Michael rushed all those words in one breath. One sweet, precious breath that told Jess everything she needed to know. Michael loved her. Michael wanted her. She felt something inside shift. Something that told her everything was going to be okay.

Throwing herself at Michael, she began to sob. "I love you too."

"Say it again," Michael begged in a whisper, her eyes as dark as night, as she pulled Jess close.

"I love you, Michael. I've been so stupid. I don't know what took me so long."

"I don't care about that. I don't care about anything but being with you. Always."

Michael smiled as she put her hands on Jess's cheeks and gently pressed their lips together. Their breath mingling. Their tears mingling. They were together at last, as they should be. And neither of them was going to let go.

EPILOGUE

Michael concentrated on the smooth lines of Jess's waist and hip wrapped up in a sheet. She quickly sketched the outline of her body. Sitting naked and cross legged on the floor near the window, sketchpad balanced on her leg, Michael was determined to get the lines right before Jess woke.

They had only been home from New York for four weeks, and Michael was distressed at the idea of Jess returning to school today where she couldn't see her, touch her, or make love to her any time she wanted. They hadn't been apart since the night her sculpture was revealed at *La Femme*, and Michael hated to see their precious time together end. Jess would return to work, and Michael would be starting on a new commission next week. Camille said she was fighting offers off with a stick. Michael was on her way to succeeding in her dream—sculpting strong, fierce woman and creating a vision for thousands to see and admire. Yet her success in work paled in comparison to the joy she felt at having Jess by her side.

The time since the opening had been the happiest period of Michael's life. She was able to be with Jess in a way she hadn't even let herself imagine before. They were still best friends as always, but there was now a layer of love and trust that took Michael's breath away. And of course, the nearly nonstop sex had her exhausted, spent, and deliriously happy. Jess's appetite for sex both surprised and delighted her. They couldn't keep their hands off each other, making up for lost time. Two weeks ago they had even messed around in the bathroom at Morgan's apartment during Girls Night In. Michael excused herself, and as she was about to return to the living room, Jess had barged into the bathroom, backed her against the wall, and demanded that Michael make her come with her mouth. Michael had obliged. Jess was spending most nights at Michael's loft, except for two or three they had spent together at Jess's apartment. Michael didn't want it to end. Jess belonged here. With her.

Steeling herself, Michael put down her sketchpad, grabbed the red velvet box from the drawer next to her bed, and rubbed Jess's bare shoulder as she crawled under the sheet with her.

"It's too early," Jess grumbled as she pulled Michael's arm tight around her waist.

"I don't want you to leave."

"I don't think I have the energy to do anything after last night." Jess moaned softly into the pillow as she pushed her ass into Michael's crotch.

"Hey," Michael whispered.

"Sweetie, what is it?" Jess looked concerned as she turned her head to face her. "You look so serious."

With her left hand Michael grabbed Jess's fingers and slipped on the ring, never letting her eyes leave Jess's face. Michael knew Jess loved her, and she felt fairly certain she wanted a future with her, but her nerves were still on edge.

"Jess. I mean I don't want you to leave. Ever. I want you to live here with me. Or wherever you want. I want you to come home to me every day. I want to lie with you every night and spend the rest of my life making up for the time I wasted being so stupid. Please say you'll be my wife." Michael spat it out in a rush and hoped she didn't sound as nervous as she felt.

Jess's smile was as big as Michael had ever seen, her cheeks pink and her eyes wide. Michael wanted to see that smile every day. And be the cause of it.

"Yes. Yes. Yes," Jess squealed and moved to straddle Michael as she stared at the ring, a vintage art deco ring Michael bought from their favorite antique dealer. The diamond was circle cut with a square setting and the band had small, intricate detail work. It was breathtaking and unique. Just like Jess. "It's beautiful. When did you find it?"

"Last Friday when you went shopping with Morgan. I was going to wait and give it to you at Christmas when we were with Mom...but I...I just couldn't wait. I'm not waiting anymore when it comes to you."

"Well, I'm not waiting either. In one hour I have to get to work to start a new school year," Jess said, rolling her naked hips against Michael's stomach. "But I can't wait until after school for you to touch me again." Grabbing Michael's hand, she shoved it between her thighs.

Michael gasped at how wet Jess already was and slipped her fingers inside. Jess's words, her body movements, and the thought of Jess as her *wife* set loose a tidal wave of emotion and longing inside her. "My wife," Michael breathed as Jess moved against her.

About the Author

Jane Hardee lives with her partner in Chicago, Illinois. She was born in North Carolina but left the Old South to pursue a career working with children with autism. When she is not teaching, writing, or watching *Family Feud*, she is probably figuring out a design for her next tattoo. Jane suffers from middle child syndrome and is a very loving aunt to a beautiful niece.

Books Available From Bold Strokes Books

Arrested Hearts by Holly Stratimore. A reckless cop with a secret death wish and a health nut who is afraid to die might be a perfect combination for love. (978-1-62639-809-2)

Capturing Jessica by Jane Hardee. Hyperrealist sculptor Michael tries desperately to conceal the love she holds for best friend, Jess, unaware Jess's feelings for her are changing. (978-1-62639-836-8)

Counting to Zero by AJ Quinn. NSA agent Emma Thorpe and computer hacker Paxton James must learn to trust each other as they work to stop a threat clock that's rapidly counting down to zero. (978-1-62639-783-5)

Courageous Love by KC Richardson. Two women fight a devastating disease, and their own demons, while trying to fall in love. (978-1-62639-797-2)

One More Reason to Leave Orlando by Missouri Vaun. Nash Wiley thought a threesome sounded exotic and exciting, but as it turns out the reality of sleeping with two women at the same time is just really complicated. (978-1-62639-703-3)

Pathogen by Jessica L. Webb. Can Dr. Kate Morrison navigate a deadly virus and the threat of bioterrorism, as well as her new relationship with Sergeant Andy Wyles and her own troubled past? (978-1-62639-833-7)

Rainbow Gap by Lee Lynch. Jaudon Vickers and Berry Garland, polar opposites, dream and love in this tale of lesbian lives set in Central Florida against the tapestry of societal change and the Vietnam War. (978-1-62639-799-6)

Steel and Promise by Alexa Black. Lady Nivrai's cruel desires and modified body make most of the galaxy fear her, but courtesan Cailyn Derys soon discovers the real monsters are the ones without the claws. (978-1-62639-805-4)

Swelter by D. Jackson Leigh. Teal Giovanni's mistake shines an unwanted spotlight on a small Texas ranch where August Reese is secluded until she can testify against a powerful drug kingpin. (978-1-62639-795-8)

Without Justice by Carsen Taite. Cade Kelly and Emily Sinclair must battle each other in the pursuit of justice, but can they fight their undeniable attraction outside the walls of the courtroom? (978-1-62639-560-2)

21 Questions by Mason Dixon. To find love, start by asking the right questions. (978-1-62639-724-8)

A Palette for Love by Charlotte Greene. When newly minted Ph.D. Chloé Devereaux returns to New Orleans, she doesn't expect her new job and her powerful employer—Amelia Winters—to be so appealing. (978-1-62639-758-3)

By the Dark of Her Eyes by Cameron MacElvee. When Brenna Taylor inherits a decrepit property haunted by tormented ghosts, Alejandra Santana must not only restore Brenna's house and property but also save her soul. (978-1-62639-834-4)

Cash Braddock by Ashley Bartlett. Cash Braddock just wants to hang with her cat, fall in love, and deal drugs. What's the problem with that? (978-1-62639-706-4)

Death by Cocktail Straw by Missouri Vaun. She just wanted to meet girls, but an outing at the local lesbian bar goes comically off the rails, landing Nash Wiley and her best pal in the ER. (978-1-62639-702-6)

Lone Ranger by VK Powell. Reporter Emma Ferguson stirs up a thirty-year-old mystery that threatens Park Ranger Carter West's family and jeopardizes any hope for a relationship between the two women. (978-1-62639-767-5)

Never Enough by Robyn Nyx. Can two women put aside their pasts to find love before it's too late? (978-1-62639-629-6)

Love on Call by Radclyffe. Ex-Army medic Glenn Archer and recent LA transplant Mariana Mateo fight their mutual desire in the face of past losses as they work together in the Rivers Community Hospital ER. (978-1-62639-843-6)

Two Souls by Kathleen Knowles. Can love blossom in the wake of tragedy? (978-1-62639-641-8)

Camp Rewind by Meghan O'Brien. A summer camp for grown-ups becomes the site of an unlikely romance between a shy, introverted divorcee and one of the Internet's most infamous cultural critics—who attends undercover. (978-1-62639-793-4)

Cross Purposes by Gina L. Dartt. In pursuit of a lost Acadian treasure, three women must work out not only the clues, but also the complicated tangle of emotion and attraction developing between them. (978-1-62639-713-2)

Imperfect Truth by C.A. Popovich. Can an imperfect truth stand in the way of love? (978-1-62639-787-3)

Life in Death by M. Ullrich. Sometimes the devastating end is your only chance for a new beginning. (978-1-62639-773-6)

Love on Liberty by MJ Williamz. Hearts collide when politics clash. (978-1-62639-639-5)

Serious Potential by Maggie Cummings. Pro golfer Tracy Allen plans to forget her ex during a visit to Bay West, a lesbian condo community in NYC, but when she meets Dr. Jennifer Betsy, she gets more than she bargained for. (978-1-62639-633-3)

Taste by Kris Bryant. Accomplished chef Taryn has walked away from her promising career in the city's top restaurant to devote her life to her six-year-old daughter and is content until Ki Blake comes along. (978-1-62639-718-7)

Valley of Fire by Missouri Vaun. Taken captive in a desert outpost after their small aircraft is hijacked, Ava and her captivating passenger discover things about each other and themselves that will change them both forever. (978-1-62639-496-4)

The Second Wave by Jean Copeland. Can star-crossed lovers have a second chance after decades apart, or does the love of a lifetime only happen once? (978-1-62639-830-6)

Coils by Barbara Ann Wright. A modern young woman follows her aunt into the Greek Underworld and makes a pact with Medusa to win her freedom by killing a hero of legend. (978-1-62639-598-5)

Courting the Countess by Jenny Frame. When relationship-phobic Lady Henrietta Knight starts to care about housekeeper Annie Brannigan and her daughter, can she overcome her fears and promise Annie the forever that she demands? (978-1-62639-785-9)

Dapper by Jenny Frame. Amelia Honey meets the mysterious Byron De Brek and is faced with her darkest fantasies, but will her strict moral upbringing stop her from exploring what she truly wants? (978-1-62639-898-6)

Delayed Gratification: The Honeymoon by Meghan O'Brien. A dream European honeymoon turns into a winter storm nightmare involving a delayed flight, a ditched rental car, and eventually, a surprisingly happy ending. (978-1-62639-766-8)

For Money or Love by Heather Blackmore. Jessica Spaulding must choose between ignoring the truth to keep everything she has, and doing the right thing only to lose it all—including the woman she loves. (978-1-62639-756-9)

Hooked by Jaime Maddox. With the help of sexy Detective Mac Calabrese, Dr. Jessica Benson is working hard to overcome her past, but they may not be enough to stop a murderer. (978-1-62639-689-0)

Lands End by Jackie D. Public relations superstar Amy Kline is dealing with a media nightmare, and the last thing she expects is for restaurateur Lena Michaels to change everything, but she will. (978-1-62639-739-2)

Bitter Root by Laydin Michaels. Small town chef Adi Bergeron is hiding something, and Griffith McNaulty is going to find out what it is even if it gets her killed. (978-1-62639-656-2)

Capturing Forever by Erin Dutton. When family pulls Jacqueline and Casey back together, will the lessons learned in eight years apart be enough to mend the mistakes of the past? (978-1-62639-631-9)

Deception by VK Powell. DEA Agent Colby Vincent and Attorney Adena Weber are embroiled in a drug investigation involving homeless veterans and an attraction that could destroy them both. (978-1-62639-596-1)

Dyre: A Knight of Spirit and Shadows by Rachel E. Bailey. With the abduction of her queen, werewolf-bodyguard Des must follow the kidnappers' trail to Europe, where her queen—and a battle unlike any Des has ever waged—awaits her. (978-1-62639-664-7)

First Position by Melissa Brayden. Love and rivalry take center stage for Anastasia Mikhelson and Natalie Frederico in one of the most prestigious ballet companies in the nation. (978-1-62639-602-9)

Best Laid Plans by Jan Gayle. Nicky and Lauren are meant for each other, but Nicky's haunting past and Lauren's societal fears threaten to derail all possibilities of a relationship. (978-1-62639-658-6)

Exchange by CF Frizzell. When Shay Maguire rode into rural Montana, she never expected to meet the woman of her dreams—or to learn Mel Baker was held hostage by legal agreement to her right-wing father. (978-1-62639-679-1)

Just Enough Light by AJ Quinn. Will a serial killer's return to Colorado destroy Kellen Ryan and Dana Kingston's chance at love, or can the search-and-rescue team save themselves? (978-1-62639-685-2)